Three Girls
in the City
CLOSE-UP

By Jeanne
Betancourt

D0566704

SCHOLASTIC INC.
New York Toronto London Auckland Sydney
Mexico City New Delhi Hong Kong Buenos Aires

DEDICATION
This book is dedicated with love to a new city girl:
PILAR BETANCOURT-POOR

ACKNOWLEDGMENTS
Thank you to Shira Golding, Kibra Yohannes, Manuela Soares, and Adriana X. Tatum for their insightful reading of this story and helpful editorial suggestions.

Three cheers go to Kate Egan and my editor, Maria Weisbin, for having the idea for Three Girls in the City in the first place.

ISBN 0-439-49842-2

4 5 6 7 8 9/0

12 11 10 9 8 7 6 5 4 3 2

Cover and interior designed by Joyce White

40

Printed in the U.S.A.
First printing, August 2004

TABLE OF CONTENTS

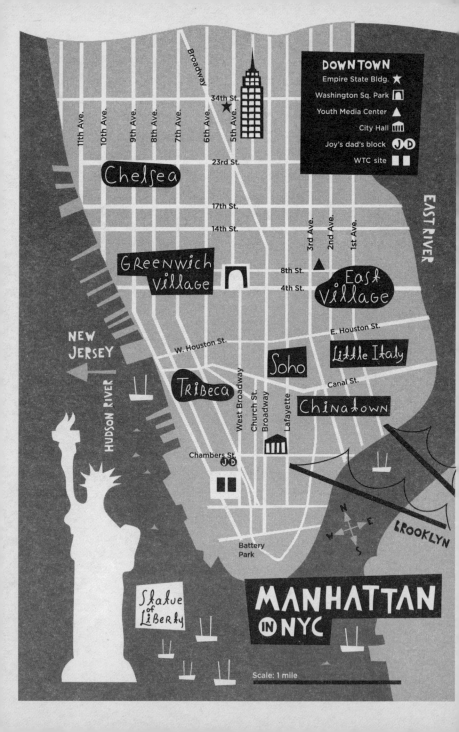

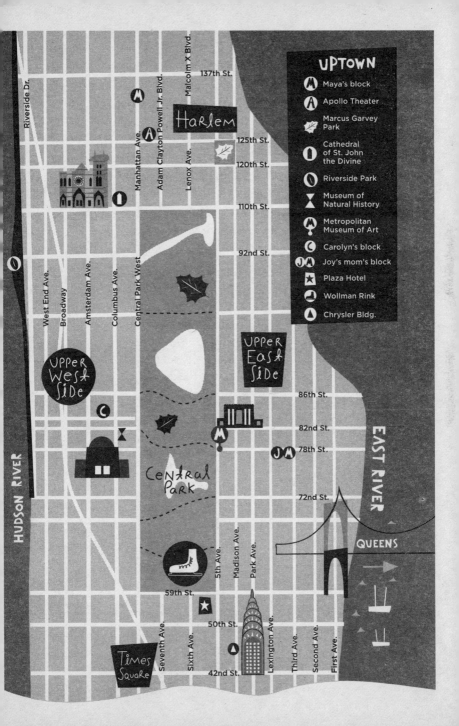

Kennedy Airport

Carolyn Kuhlberg woke to a voice from her clock radio. "With the humidity, it'll feel like one hundred degrees. It's going to be a hot, sticky day for New York City!"

Carolyn opened her eyes and thought, It's going to be a great day for me. Photography workshop starts today and Mandy is coming for two weeks.

As warm shower water soaked Carolyn's head and slipped over her body, she thought about what to wear. By the time she was back to her room she'd made up her mind. Denim shorts, red high-top sneakers, and her new sleeveless T. It was pale green with pink sequins across the front that spelled out COWGIRL.

Now that I live in the city, am I still a cowgirl? Carolyn wondered as she pulled on the shirt. Joy and Maya — her best friends in New York — would like it. She could count on Joy to make a sarcastic comment, but not to be mean. Sarcasm was just part of Joy's sense of humor. If there were a T-shirt for Joy, Carolyn thought, it would say RICH GIRL. Of course Joy would never wear a top that said that. Joy didn't show off or brag that her parents were rich. In fact, Carolyn noticed that sometimes Joy tried to hide it. She remembered the time she and Maya saw Joy getting out of a cab two blocks away from the media center. "Why didn't she take the cab all the way?" she'd asked Maya. Maya said Joy probably didn't want everyone to know she could afford to take cabs.

Carolyn sat across from her father at the kitchen counter and poured milk into a bowl of cereal with sliced banana. He handed her a section of the newspaper. "Mandy's coming tonight," she reminded him.

He looked at her over his reading glasses. "We should leave for the airport by five. Maxine is lending me her car."

Carolyn tried to swallow the cereal in her mouth, but it stuck halfway down. Maxine? Maxine Geng — her father's former girlfriend. The woman she called M. G. Carolyn managed to swallow and sputter, "I thought you broke up with her, I mean, didn't she break up with you or something like that? Because her boyfriend —"

Her father held up a hand to stop her. "Hold on. Dr. Geng and I are just friends and colleagues. She is an entomologist, too, you know. We're working on a project together. She's doing us a favor by lending us her car."

"Right," agreed Carolyn. She knew in her brain that her dad needed a grown-up woman in his life. A girlfriend. Enough time had passed since her mother had died. But she didn't want someone trying to replace her. Especially if that someone was M. G.

Her father stood up and kissed her on the forehead. "I have to go to work, honey. I'll be back here by four. It will be good for you to have Mandy here. You two must miss each other."

We do miss each other, Carolyn thought as she finished up her breakfast. She couldn't wait to see her oldest, best friend.

A few minutes later, Carolyn walked out of her apartment building. She was met by a blast of summer city heat and Ivy George walking six dogs.

Ivy grinned at Carolyn. "Hey, Red. Just the girl I wanted to see."

Carolyn grinned back. She liked Ivy. Ivy was almost as old as her dad, but she acted a lot younger and was super hip. She had short, spiked hair, a tattoo around her wrist, and was a drummer with her own band — the Big Bang Band. Carolyn loved their music.

One of the dogs — a boxer — pulled on his leash.

Ivy gave the leash a little tug and said firmly, "Jax, stay." Jax did.

"I never saw that dog before," said Carolyn.

Ivy looked around at the dogs. "I have three new ones to walk," she explained. "Jax here. Then there's Gertrude." She pointed to a standard poodle. "And that pug next to her. Tyson."

"That's a lot of dogs to walk."

"It is," agreed Ivy. "The new ones are from the

building next door. You want a summer job helping me walk dogs? I could use help. Especially in the mornings. That's when I have the most."

"I'd love to!" exclaimed Carolyn.

Precious — a Great Dane the size of a pony — nudged Carolyn's hand with his nose. She massaged his velvety forehead with her thumb. "But I have photo workshop from ten to one on Tuesday and Thursday. That's where I'm going now."

"We can work around your schedule," said Ivy. "We'll just start a little earlier."

Carolyn suddenly remembered the one person who could stand between her and a summer job. "I'll have to ask my dad."

"Not to worry," Ivy told her. "I saw him just a minute ago and checked it out. He said it was okay as long as you're not walking dogs alone in the park, which you won't be."

Carolyn felt excited and annoyed in the same instant. Excited to have a job, especially with Ivy. Annoyed that her dad said she couldn't walk dogs alone in the park. That was embarrassing.

"Do you want me to watch the new dogs while you bring the others back to their apartments?" she asked Ivy.

"Don't you have to get to that workshop?"

Carolyn glanced at her watch. "I have time."

"Okay," Ivy agreed. "By the way, nice T-shirt."

Carolyn gave Precious a final pat, and Ivy led

him and his pals inside. Jax barked a where-are-you-going-without-me bark at the departing dogs and tried to follow.

"It's okay, Jax," Carolyn said with a little tug on his leash. "Stay."

He did.

This is so great! Carolyn thought. I have a summer job with animals. I love animals! Mandy can help me. She loves animals, too. The next thought clouded Carolyn's happiness. *Will Mandy like Ivy? Or will she be put off by Ivy's tattoo and out-there city style? And what if Mandy doesn't like Joy and Maya? I didn't like Joy when I first met her.* The next thought came on quickly. *What if Joy and Maya don't like Mandy?*

As Maya Johnson opened the front door of her Harlem brownstone, she realized that she'd forgotten her subway pass. She headed back up the two flights of stairs to her room.

She was halfway up the second flight when she heard her sister Naomi's voice. "We're not supposed to be in Maya's room when she's not here, Hannah. She said."

"Only 'cause she doesn't understand," protested Hannah.

Maya stood in the doorway and asked loudly, "What don't I understand?"

Naomi jumped with surprise, but nine-year-old Hannah continued rummaging through Maya's box of hair dressing supplies. "You don't understand that I need these for my business," she said. "I'll pay you back, Maya. I promise."

Maya looked down in the box to see if anything important was already missing. Her favorite leopard-print scrunchie, and red-black-and-green–striped barrettes were still there.

"She's going to fix Anika's hair — at day camp," Naomi explained.

Hannah held up a card of ten bright-pink butterfly barrettes. "Can I have these? You never even use them."

"The butterfly ones?!" wailed Naomi. "I wanted those for *my* hair."

"But you don't pay, Naomi," Hannah explained patiently. "Anika will pay."

"Okay, Hannah," agreed Maya. "You can have them. But give two to Naomi. Now go on, guys. Mom's waiting to take you to day camp."

Maya checked her reflection in the mirror over her bureau. Hannah had put a dozen or so braids with red beads in her hair. They looked good with her gray tank top and khaki capris. Hannah was pretty good at doing hair. Maya scanned the top of her bureau. No MetroCard. What was I wearing the last time I used it? she wondered. My jeans, she remembered as she looked around the room for them. They were draped over her desk chair. The MetroCard was in the back pocket. She took it and ran down the stairs.

Her mother was standing at the front door helping five-year-old Naomi rearrange the things in her backpack. Hannah and Piper — the youngest of the four sisters — were sitting on the bottom step. Hannah was adding the card of butterfly barrettes to her shoe box of hair salon supplies. Piper was opening and closing the Velcro straps on her new sandals.

Maya stepped over the shoe box. "I need to get through here, guys. I'm late."

Their mother stopped Maya with a hand on her shoulder. "Can you come to the store this afternoon? Around three. I need help unpacking a new shipment."

Maya thought quickly through her day. Workshop until one. Have to be on the subway by two-fifteen to get to the store by three. That leaves an hour and fifteen minutes to hang out with Carolyn and Joy after the workshop. "Okay, Mom," she agreed.

Piper grabbed Maya's hand. "I wanna go with my May-a."

Maya and her mother exchanged a glance. "You could drop her off at nursery school on the way to the subway," her mother said. "It would help me out here."

"Okay," agreed Maya. She patted her littlest sister on the head. "But you have to walk fast, Pipe."

As Maya helped Piper down the front steps she thought, at least I get paid for taking care of my sisters. And for working at the store. Joy babysits a lot for her half brother, Jake, but she doesn't get paid for it. I guess it doesn't make any difference to her. Her parents give her all the money she wants.

Joy Benoit-Cohen knocked on her mother's bedroom door.

"What?" her mother called out in a groggy voice.

Joy opened the door. The drapes were still drawn. Her mother sat up in bed. "Where you going, honey?"

"To photo workshop. The summer session starts today. I need a check to pay for it."

Her mother poked bare feet into slippers. "You'll have to get it from your father."

"He paid last time," protested Joy. "It's your turn."

"Look, Joy, I told you business is flat. Your father is just going to have to pick up the slack."

"But —" Joy protested.

"He's rolling in dough," her mother added.

No he's not, Joy thought as she went back to her own room. Not anymore. When was her father going to tell her mother that he had lost his job? And when was her mother going to tell him that she hardly had any television commercials to produce? Sometimes it was hard to keep her number one rule for being a kid of divorced parents: *Stay out of the middle. Don't talk about one parent to the other parent.*

Joy looked down at her feet and thought, Loafers and socks are way too warm for today. I should wear sandals. She felt the strip of belly exposed between her stretchy white T-shirt and hip-hugger denim skirt. Was her belly too big for this style? She pulled the shirt down to meet the waist of her skirt. It sprung back up. Oh, well, she thought. Who cares? And if somebody does care, who cares if they care? I don't.

She slipped a new board book for Jake into her backpack. Next, she checked her wallet for cash. Not much of last week's allowance left after buying the book. She hoped her mother would at least give her a few dollars to get through the day.

Her mother was back in bed with a cup of coffee and *The New York Times*.

"Don't you have to go to the office, Mom?" Joy asked. "It's, like, nine-thirty."

Her mother finally looked up. "I'll get there."

"I need some money," Joy said. "To buy lunch and stuff."

"Of course you do." She pointed at her easy chair with her pencil. "In my wallet. Take five. That should hold you until you get your allowance from your father. You're babysitting there today, aren't you?"

"Un-huh," Joy agreed. She took the money out of her mother's wallet.

Going down in the elevator a few minutes later, Joy thought about how just a few months ago she had a big allowance and a credit card, too. In those good old days, sometimes both her parents would give her a weekly allowance.

The doorman smiled as he opened the front door, "Would you like a cab today, Miss Benoit?"

"Not today, Frederick," she answered as she stepped out into the hot day. She headed down the block toward the subway station.

Carolyn had been waiting for the subway for five steamy minutes when a train finally pulled into the station. She ran up to the third car from the front, as usual. That's the car she and Maya always rode in so that if they were on the same train they could go to the workshop together. Maya won't be on this train though, she thought as she stepped into the car. I'm really late.

But Maya was there, sitting in the middle of the air-conditioned car, reading the newspaper. Carolyn stood in front of her and kneed the paper.

Maya looked up, surprised. "I thought you already went. How come you're late?"

"I got a job!" Carolyn exclaimed, remembering her good news.

The train stopped at the 72nd Street station, and the man next to Maya got off. Carolyn took his seat. She told Maya all about her job and the new dogs.

They were still talking about the job when Maya interrupted to say, "This train isn't moving."

Carolyn looked around. They were still in the 72nd Street station. The subway car was stuffed with people getting on during the long delay. Finally, the doors closed. As the train lurched forward, a woman standing over Carolyn teetered toward her. The man grabbed the woman's arm to keep her from falling.

Carolyn noticed that he was holding a map. A guide-book to New York City was stuck in the side of the purse the woman clutched to her chest.

Tourists, decided Carolyn. I bet this is the first time they've taken a subway and they're a little afraid. That's how I felt when I took the subway for the first time. Mandy will feel that way, too. We're so much alike. She smiled to herself, remembering how she and Mandy used to pretend they were sisters. We weren't afraid of riding for hours on the open range or sleeping overnight under the stars, she thought. But it took time for me to be comfortable in the big crowded city. That's how it will be for Mandy.

The train was held up in the next station and the one after that. While they were waiting at the 59th Street stop, Carolyn caught the tourist woman looking at her, a worried expression still on her face. Carolyn smiled and said, "This always happens." The woman smiled back.

At 42nd Street / Times Square, the tourist couple got off and Carolyn and Maya changed trains.

It was another fifteen minutes before they reached Eighth Street.

"We're already late," Maya told Carolyn as they stepped out of the subway car.

Carolyn tugged on Maya's bag. "Serge is right over there! By the trash can."

Maya saw him — bleached hair, spiked and tipped with blue. When he saw them looking at him, a big grin spread across his face.

As they walked toward Serge, Carolyn did a quick count of his face jewelry. Only two today. Nose and right eyebrow. She remembered when she first saw Serge. He'd had five rings and studs in his face and had been just another interesting-looking person crossing Second Avenue. Now he was a friend.

They smiled their hellos and Maya held out her newspaper. "Want it?"

Serge took it. "I have a newspaper for you, too."

Even in a short sentence like that, Carolyn could hear Serge's Russian accent.

"This is my train," he shouted above the screech and roar of a train pulling into the station. "I miss two trains waiting for you." He thrust his paper into Carolyn's hand and rushed toward the opening doors of the train.

The first time Maya saw Serge was on this same subway platform. He'd picked up the newspaper she left on the edge of the trash can. He'd taken her paper the next time she left one, too. After that, she and Carolyn and Joy put a note for him in the paper. Just for the fun of it. They'd done it lots.

Maya looked down at the paper he'd just given Carolyn. It was in Russian.

Carolyn opened the paper to the centerfold. Serge had written them a note in bright red letters.

I HAVE HOUR TO SEE YOU AFTER CAMERA CLASS. MEET ME AT CORNER OF SECOND AVENUE. ONE O'CLOCK. BE THERE OR BE SQUARE. SERGE.

"Be there or be square?" laughed Carolyn. "Where did he learn that?"

"Should we tell him it's sort of a lame thing to say?" Maya asked as they ran up the stairs to the street.

"Nah. That'll make him self-conscious. Besides, when *he* says stuff like that, it's sort of cute."

"You're so sweet, CK," Maya said.

Even though it was hot and sticky out, they ran the rest of the way to the media center.

Joy was already there. She flipped through the books of photos that Beth had left on the workshop table and wished that Maya and Carolyn would hurry up and get there. A worried thought popped into her head. What if one of them had decided not to take the summer workshop? Wouldn't they have called and told her? Or would they just not show up and let her figure it out for herself? Maya and Carolyn were closer to each other than either of them was to her. If only one of them took the workshop, which one would I want it to be? Joy wondered. Maya is sophisticated and city smart. But Carolyn is so sweet and fun to be with. A horrible thought pushed the decision of which friend to choose right out of Joy's head. *What if Carolyn and Maya both dropped out of the workshop?*

Beth came over to her. Sometimes Joy thought Beth was a great photography teacher. Other times she wasn't so sure.

13

"I have good news," Beth said. "A corporate sponsor donated two computers and Photoshop to the media center. You can use it."

"I have Photoshop at home," Joy reminded her.

"By *you*, I meant everyone in the class," Beth explained. "We'll all be using digital cameras this summer. Got those donated, too."

"You can edit regular photos in Photoshop," Joy pointed out. "They don't have to be digital. You just scan them in."

"I know that much," Beth said with an edgy laugh. "But you're right, there's a lot I don't know about digital. I'm learning, though. Anyway, I might call on you to help the others. Is that okay with you?"

"Sure," agreed Joy. "Why not?"

She heard someone come in and looked toward the door. It wasn't Maya or Carolyn but a guy she'd never seen before.

Sometimes Maya's a few minutes late, Joy thought. She lives farther uptown than Carolyn and has her sisters to take care of. But Carolyn's never late.

"Where are your pals, Joy?" Beth asked. "I want to get started here."

Joy shrugged her shoulders.

At that moment Maya and Carolyn came running in. They saw Joy and headed straight toward her.

Joy relaxed. Nothing had changed. They were all there. The three of them together again.

"Let's go," Beth called. "Everyone take a seat around the table."

Maya reached the table first and saved a place on either side for Carolyn and Joy. She looked around to see who else was taking the summer workshop. Janice was across from her. She'd taken all the workshops so far. And Jennifer and Max from the last workshop. There was a new boy sitting at the end of the table. His skin is darker than mine, thought Maya. Good. I'm not the only black person in the workshop.

When Joy sat down, Maya put the Russian newspaper in front of her and opened it to the centerfold.

Joy read it quickly and laughed. "Be there or be square? That sounds so corny."

Carolyn grinned at her. "Exactly."

"Let's not waste any more time, people," Beth scolded. "All eyes up here, please."

Joy imagined them all taking out their eyeballs and rolling them like marbles along the tabletop to Beth. She glanced at Carolyn sitting at attention, ready to be a good student of photography. Carolyn would never have a weird thought like that.

"So you are all present and accounted for," continued Beth. She gestured toward the new boy. "Everyone, this is Ousmane." Ousmane smiled at each of them and nodded as Beth said everyone's name.

He's very formal, thought Carolyn. I wonder where he's from.

Maya was wondering the same thing and guessed from his name that he was probably from West Africa.

Joy wasn't thinking about Ousmane. She was wondering where Charlie was. Even though Charlie had some disease that was causing him to slowly go blind, he'd taken all the photography workshops so far. "Where's Charlie?" she asked Beth.

"He's gone to a special camp for kids with vision problems. He's planning on taking the fall workshop, though."

Maya, Carolyn, and Joy exchanged a glance. They liked Charlie and would miss him.

Beth explained that they'd be shooting digital and learning some basic Photoshop techniques. "What's the difference between the single-lens reflex cameras most of you have been using and digital cameras," she asked. "Joy?"

"You don't use film," answered Joy. "You have cards that store the data digitally. If you transfer the information from the card into a computer, you can edit your photos. You can even print them out from your computer or have them printed at a regular developing place. Whatever you want to do."

"Right," agreed Beth. "How's it different when you're taking pictures?"

"First of all, you don't have to look through the eyepiece," began Joy. "You can see what you're shooting on this LCD screen that makes everything look like it's on television. It's really freeing not to have the camera up to your face."

Beth passed around cameras, and they all

turned them on and looked at one another on the LCD screens to check out the television effect.

"There's also a time lag with digital," Joy continued, "so the picture you record is what happens a little after you press the button. But you get used to it.

They all took pictures of one another to see what she meant.

Then Joy demonstrated some of the cool things they could do with Photoshop using the pictures they'd taken. Everyone cracked up when she superimposed Beth's face on Ousmane's body.

Beth asked them how they could represent dreams or memories using Photoshop. Jennifer said that having one image oversized in a picture would make the scene seem like a nightmare. Maya said that sometimes memories seem a little out of focus.

"Being out of focus is like dreams, too," added Ousmane. "And using odd colors."

"You're on the right track," agreed Beth. "So think dream and memory using the digital cameras and Photoshop. You can also scan in old pictures if that helps. Your assignment this summer is to make images that are otherworldly."

"Otherworldly?" Joy whispered to Maya. "I have enough trouble with this world."

"Yeah, I know what you mean," Maya whispered back. But I don't have as much trouble with the real world as Joy does, Maya thought. Even though she's super smart, pretty, and rich, she seems really sad sometimes.

Carolyn remembered a dream she'd had the night before. Riding alone in the hills behind the ranch. She saw another rider up ahead — a woman. The woman turned in the saddle and smiled. It was her mother. Mom's back, she thought as she galloped to catch up. She galloped and galloped. But she never could reach her mother. She woke up crying.

Can I make that dream a photograph? she wondered. A lump of tears rose in her throat. It would be too painful to even try.

Beth opened her attendance book. "I need checks, people. I'm collecting. Then it's hasta la vista until Thursday. Think pictures."

"I didn't know she spoke Spanish," Carolyn told Joy.

"Oh, CK," Joy said. "I worry about you."

Carolyn smiled a just-kidding grin at her. But Joy wasn't so sure.

Carolyn gave Beth a check.

Maya told Beth that her mother mailed hers.

Joy said, "Mine did, too." And they left.

Maya loved that they were meeting up with Serge. The four of them bought falafel sandwiches from a cart and went to Astor Place — a small patch of pavement where Eighth Street, Lafayette Street, and Fourth Avenue intersected. They sat under the big black metal cube sculpture to eat. A Chilean band was playing nearby. The music from a guitar, reed flute, and clarinet was bright and light above the hum and honks of traffic.

"Carolyn's friend is coming tonight," Joy told Serge. "She'll be here for a couple weeks."

Serge pointed his soda can at Carolyn's T-shirt. "She is cowgirl like you?"

"We used to ride together all the time," Carolyn answered.

"I meant to tell you I *love* your T-shirt," teased Joy. She saw worry wrinkle Carolyn's forehead. "Just kidding. I do like it."

"Me, too," agreed Maya. "Did you have cows on the ranch, CK?"

"I rustled cattle," answered Carolyn in her best western twang. She raised her arm and drew a big circle around her head. "And we lasso. So watch out."

"You do?" said Joy, surprised.

Carolyn nodded. "Mandy, too. We grew up doing that stuff."

"What's Mandy like?" asked Maya.

"Quiet. Nice. She's a great rider. A year older than me. But it never seemed that way. She's sort of innocent."

Joy arched an eyebrow.

"I mean, like, she's never been to the city," Carolyn added quickly. She showed them a picture of Mandy that she kept in her wallet.

Mandy in jeans and a flannel shirt. Her brown hair in two ponytails. Grinning at the camera.

"She loves animals," Carolyn continued. "I think walking dogs in Central Park in the morning will help her get adjusted to being in the city. When I first moved here —"

Joy put a hand on her arm and whispered, "Look at that guy in the muscle-T. He's going to pass us. I've seen him before. Check out the tattoo on his arm."

As the guy passed, Carolyn saw the tattoo. DEB-BIE was written in red script. And crossed out. Under it was a heart with SANDY in it. The whole heart was crossed out. Under that was written MELODY.

"Unlucky in love," said Maya when he'd passed.

"And tattoos," added Joy.

"That tells me something," Serge said. "I must go to work at tattoo and piercing parlor. You walk me?"

Maya checked her watch. "I have to go, Serge. I'm working at my mom's store this afternoon."

"And I have to get ready for Mandy," said Carolyn, getting up. She smiled at Maya. "I'll take the subway with you."

Serge gave the cube a little push to turn it and looked at Joy. "You come with me?"

Her stomach turned a flip. I've never been alone with Serge, she realized. Just me and Serge. She stood up and said, "I can't, either," even though she could have. She pulled her T-shirt down over her exposed belly.

Carolyn and her father were waiting at the airport arrival gate for Flight 472. The plane had landed.

Her heart thumped. *Mandy is coming. Mandy is coming.* Dozens of people streamed through the exit gate. A man greeted a woman with balloons. I should have thought of that for Mandy, thought Carolyn. She held on to her father's arm to balance on tiptoe to look for Mandy. Where was she?

An older girl with short, bleached hair, wearing a black miniskirt, denim halter top, and red cowboy boots, was waving at her.

"I'm here!" exclaimed the girl. She ran forward and hugged Carolyn.

Mandy?! thought Carolyn as she hugged her back.

Empire State Building

After hugging Dr. Kuhlberg hello, Mandy looked around and happily exclaimed, "Hello, New York!"

"Mandy. I — I didn't even recognize you," Carolyn said. "Your hair —"

But Mandy wasn't listening. She'd turned to a handsome young man who came up beside her. "It was great meeting you, Mandy," he said. "Have fun in New York."

"I will," she promised. "Thanks."

As the guy continued through the gate, Dr. Kuhlberg asked Mandy, "Do you know him?"

"He sat next to me on the plane," she explained. "He told me lots of stuff to do in New York."

"I see," said Dr. Kuhlberg. "Well, when you're here, Mandy, you shouldn't talk to strangers. It's a little different here than in Dubois."

"Okay," agreed Mandy. "I won't." She rolled her eyes at Carolyn behind his back.

Mandy's not going to be following Dad's rules for city living, Carolyn thought.

Half an hour later they were driving back to the

city. Carolyn took the backseat so Mandy could sit up front and have a good view.

As they went over the Queensboro Bridge, the city skyline stretched before them. "There's the Empire State Building!" Mandy announced excitedly. "I definitely want to go there." She turned to Carolyn in the backseat. "It's first on my list." She faced forward again and asked, "Where did the World Trade Center used to be?"

"Look to your left," Dr. K directed. "It was way downtown. To your right is uptown."

"Ground Zero," said Mandy solemnly. "I have to go there." She turned toward Carolyn again. "One of your friends saw the whole thing from her bedroom. Right?"

"Joy did," answered Carolyn.

"I want to ask her about that on tape," Mandy said as she went back to looking out the front window.

"Joy doesn't —" Carolyn started to say.

Mandy interrupted her. "There's the Chrysler Building! That's on my list, too. We should check out the lobby. It's supposed to be gorgeous. I'll put it in my video."

Carolyn leaned forward. "What video?"

"You'll never guess," answered Mandy. "I took a video production course at the public-access station back home. They put great stuff on the air. And they have this whole thing going on with youth media. I told them I wanted to make a movie about New York City, and they lent me a great camera. And if my tape's good enough, they'll put it on the air. How cool is that?"

"Pretty cool," agreed Carolyn. Mandy hadn't told her about the course. They hadn't e-mailed much in the last few months. There was a lot of news about Mandy that she had missed. Like she dyed her hair, totally changed the way she dressed, and went from being shy to talking to cute older guys on planes.

As Joy crossed the street to Mario's Restaurant and Pizzeria she reviewed the two big topics she wanted to discuss with her father during dinner. First, she'd tell him that she wanted to go back to living with him. Maybe for the whole summer. The second topic was about babysitting Jake. Instead of getting an allowance, she wanted to be paid for taking care of him. She'd be sure to tell her dad that she wouldn't charge as much as a regular sitter. And one more thing I have to bring up, she remembered. I have to ask him for half of the money for the workshop. He and Mom should split it. Isn't that what "joint custody" means?

Her father was already in a booth near the front of the restaurant. She slipped into the seat across from him before he even noticed her.

"Hi," he said when he looked up. "Hungry?"

"I am," she answered.

The sweet, tangy smell of tomato sauce made

her mouth water. They'd walked by this restaurant a lot but had never eaten there. Her father liked to eat at fancier, more expensive places. Dad can't afford those places anymore, Joy thought. He must hate that.

"I've always wanted to eat here, Dad," she said. "I love Italian."

He was already looking at the menu. "I'm going for spaghetti and meatballs."

She scanned the menu. "Lasagna for me."

"I have news, Joy," he said suddenly.

"You got a job?" she guessed.

"No. Sorry to say. Quite the opposite." The waiter interrupted them to take their order. Ideas of what bad news her father might have ran through Joy's head. He and Sue had been fighting a lot since he lost his job. Were they separating? Joy didn't like Sue very much, but she didn't want them to get divorced. For Jake's sake. But what else could it be? What if her father was sick? Really sick — like Carolyn's mother had been.

Joy studied her father's face. He looked pale and had dark circles under his eyes. She swallowed the lump rising in her throat. Sometimes she didn't like her father very much, but she sure didn't want him to be sick. Or die.

As soon as the waiter left, Joy leaned forward and asked, "What's the news, Dad? Is it really bad?"

"Not bad for you." He took a sip of water before adding, "We're moving to a two-bedroom place farther downtown. Sue and I — and Jake, of course. It's in a nice enough building, though it's nothing like where we are now. But the apartment is half the price. Which is the point."

Two bedrooms. One for her father and Sue. The second one for Jake. "I won't have a bedroom there?" she asked.

"Well, the truth is that you're with your mother most of the time now and your room at my place wasn't being used."

"Sue has her exercise machine in there," Joy reminded him.

"Well, Sue is going to have to make sacrifices, too," he said sharply. "Anyway, we'll get one of those air mattresses for when you stay over, or you can stay on the pullout couch in the living room. I'm sorry, Joy."

"That's okay, Dad," she said, even though it wasn't okay. How could she move back in with him if she didn't have a room? She didn't like Sue, and for a long time she didn't like having a baby brother. But she liked her room in her dad's apartment. And now she loved having a baby brother. Jake was cute and fun to be around. He loved her, too, she could tell.

Her father smiled at her with sad eyes. "You said you had something you wanted to talk to me about. What's up?"

The waiter put small salads in front of them.

"I just had an idea of how you could save some money," she answered. "On babysitting. Instead of giving me an allowance, you could pay me for taking care of Jake, but I wouldn't charge as much as your other babysitter. I can babysit a lot because it's summer vacation."

He arched an eyebrow in her direction. "Really?"

She nodded. "I'd charge, like, twenty-five percent less than the going rate."

He patted her hand and laughed. "Chip off the old block. Give me a deal I can't refuse. I save on your allowance, get a twenty-five–percent discount on babysitting, and Jake will be one-hundred percent happy. It's a deal." His smile slipped to a frown. "I'm sorry I had to take away your credit card, Joy."

"I know you are, Dad." She hesitated before adding, "Also, I need a check for half of my photography workshop fee. Mom will pay the other half."

"Didn't I pay for the last workshop?" he asked.

She nodded.

"Then ask your mother for all of it."

Mandy and Carolyn had walked all over the Upper West Side with Carolyn's father. They'd seen Lincoln Center, the mega record store, the mega-bookstore, and been window-shopping along both sides of Columbus Avenue. By midnight, Mandy's clothes were put away in the closet and in the two drawers that Carolyn had emptied out for her. Her makeup was spread across the top of the bureau. The trundle bed was pulled out and made up. Carolyn was in worn pajama bottoms and an old T-shirt.

Mandy had on a silk tiger-patterned nightgown. *Mandy?*

When they were finally in bed, Carolyn told Mandy, "I almost didn't recognize you."

"Thanks," said Mandy. "Do you like my hair?"

"It's a nice color," answered Carolyn. "It makes you look older."

"Katrina did it."

"Katrina Swenson?" asked Carolyn. "You're hanging out with her?"

"Uh-huh. Kat was in my video class."

Katrina Swenson, thought Carolyn. Older than either of them, star of the "in" clique, and the best at whatever she did.

"We're best friends now," Mandy added. "We have so much fun together."

Carolyn thought but didn't say, I'm supposed to be your best friend. Instead she changed the subject. "How's Storm?"

"I pretty much gave him to my sister," Mandy answered. "She's big enough to ride him now."

"You're not riding?"

"Don't have time. I'm always working on videos. Katrina and I had this great idea. In the fall we're going to make videos for your grandparents of horses and ponies that they are trying to sell. I'll shoot it and Katrina will do the voice-over. We'll use the sample reels to convince other ranchers to hire us. We're calling our company Mandrina Productions. Isn't that an awesome name?" She took a deep breath and added sleepily, "We'll have a Web site and everything. We already bought the domain name."

Carolyn stared at the yellow glow of her nightlight. It was shaped like a pony. She'd had it since she was little. Mandy had one, too. She remembered the day they'd spotted them at their favorite store, Horsing Around, and begged her mother to buy them.

"Do you still have your horse night-light?" she asked Mandy.

Mandy didn't answer. Carolyn heard her slow, even sleep breath and closed her own eyes.

The next morning, Carolyn woke to the sound of the hair dryer. Mandy was already showered and dressed in white pants, silver sandals, and a stretchy blue top. While she blow-dried her hair, Carolyn showered and put on a pair of jeans and a plain T-shirt. Mandy turned her attention to makeup, and Carolyn went to make their breakfast.

She came back to the room to tell Mandy it was ready. "I have to walk the dogs in a few minutes," she added. "Then Maya and Joy are going to meet us here. You don't have to walk the dogs if you don't want."

Mandy waved a mascara wand in her direction. "Of course I want to. You're going to Central Park. It's famous. Besides, I'm dying to meet Ivy. You told me so much about her."

"I did?"

"Sure. You e-mailed me about her cool apartment that's all blue and has a bathtub in the kitchen and a cemetery in the backyard. You photographed her and her band at that street fair. Right?"

"Right," agreed Carolyn. Mandy knows all about what I've been doing in New York over the last year, she thought. Why don't I know what she's been doing?

Carolyn and Mandy were waiting for Ivy when she came out of the building next door with Jax, Gertrude, and Tyson.

Mandy introduced herself to Ivy before Carolyn had a chance to do it. "I heard you're a drummer, Ivy," she said after they'd shaken hands. "I'd like to hear you play while I'm here."

Ivy smiled. "There's a free concert coming up. You should come." She looked toward Carolyn's apartment building. "I've gotta go pick up the other dogs now. I'll give you the details when I come down."

Carolyn took the three new dogs from Ivy.

"This is so perfect," Mandy exclaimed after Ivy left. "I'll tape that show."

Ivy never told *me* about the show, thought Carolyn.

Mandy brushed Jax away from her leg. "Hey, dog, these pants are white. I'd like them to stay that way."

Carolyn had a memory flash. Mandy's dog Ruff running out to greet Mandy. Mandy bending down so Ruff could give her a wet kiss. How did she turn into someone afraid a dog will mess up her pants?

*　　　*　　　*

Joy was walking through Central Park on the way to Carolyn's apartment on the West Side when she spotted Carolyn with Ivy and the dogs on one of the paths. Who's the blond with them? she wondered as she ran to catch up.

When they all met, Carolyn introduced the blond. This was Mandy, the girl whose photo Carolyn had showed her?

As they walked the dogs out of the park, Mandy told Joy, "I have my trip all planned out. Day One, I'm doing the Empire State Building. Then I want to see Times Square. After that, a walk up Fifth Avenue with stops at St. Patrick's Cathedral, Rockefeller Center, Saks Fifth Avenue, FAO Schwarz, and the Plaza Hotel."

"Good planning," observed Ivy.

"And I'm videotaping it all," concluded Mandy. She started to tell Ivy and Joy all about the video but then stopped mid-sentence to admire Ivy's wrist tattoo, which she'd just noticed.

"I have another one," said Ivy. She handed the dog leashes to Mandy and raised her shirt a few inches to expose her back. A flying eagle was tattooed just above her waistline. Joy and Carolyn exchanged a glance. Ivy had never showed them the eagle tattoo.

"My great, great grandmother was Cherokee," explained Ivy. "That's why I chose the eagle. For the Cherokee, the eagle connects earth with the spirit world."

I had forgotten that Ivy had Native American ancestors, thought Carolyn.

Carolyn, Mandy, and Joy were back in Carolyn's apartment for only a few minutes when Maya rang the downstairs buzzer. Joy went to the apartment door to let her in. She couldn't wait to see Maya's reaction to Mandy.

As Maya came up on the elevator, Maya was thinking about Mandy, too. Her old best friend, Shana, hadn't liked it when she brought her new friends around. How will Carolyn's old best friend feel about Joy and me? she wondered.

She pressed the apartment doorbell.

A girl with bleached hair, hip clothes, and careful makeup opened the door and greeted Maya with a big smile. "Hi. Come on in. I'm Mandy. I'm so happy to finally meet you." She gave Maya a hug.

Maya exchanged a glance with Joy over Mandy's shoulder. *This is Mandy?*

Before Maya could get over her surprise, Mandy announced, "Let's go. The Empire State Building opens at eight o'clock. We're already way late." She picked up a small digital video camera and quickly told Maya about her project. "You'll all be in it," she said as they walked down the hall to the elevator.

"That's great," commented Maya. "How'd you learn how to make movies?"

Mandy and Maya were still talking about the videotaping as they crossed Broadway to the subway stop.

Joy and Carolyn walked behind them.

Joy arched an eyebrow in Carolyn's direction. "Mandy's not exactly the way you described her."

"She's changed," Carolyn observed quietly.

Maya laughed at something Mandy had said.

Mandy's changed so much, thought Carolyn, I don't even know if I like her anymore.

Walking down the stairs to the subway platform, Maya took Carolyn's arm. "Mandy's great," she whispered. "I already like her. We're going to have so much fun."

I've never been to the Empire State Building, thought Carolyn. Maybe I will have fun.

And she did. The view from the 86th floor was amazing. "You have eighty miles of visibility today, folks," one of the guards told them. "It's one of the best days we've had in a long time, so enjoy it."

Joy liked being at the Empire State Building, too. She remembered going there with her uncle Brett when she was little. He had lifted her up so she could have a better view. She'd felt safe and a little scared at the same time. Uncle Brett's been dead for almost five years, she thought, and I still miss him so much.

Mandy moved in front of Joy, blocking the view and interrupting her memories. She pointed her camera to the northwest corner of the observation deck. "Joy, stand over there and look out at the view," Mandy directed. "You're going to be in this video a lot, so I want the audience to get to know you."

Before Joy could say no, Mandy turned to Maya and Carolyn. "You two get in the shot, too."

Maya and Carolyn are doing it, thought Joy. If I say no, I'll be the odd girl out.

The three friends stood side by side looking over the city toward the Hudson River and New Jersey.

"The first part will have a music overlay," Mandy explained. "Then I need a reaction shot from you guys. So when I count to three, Joy, you turn to me and say, "I love it up here. We can see forever.""

Joy said it — reluctantly.

Mandy turned off the camera. "That was good but let's try it again, with a little more enthusiasm, Joy. Okay?"

Maya thought, Joy? Enthusiasm? I don't think so.

Joy said, "I love it up here. We can see forever," one more time. But as soon as Mandy lowered the camera, Joy sent her a glare that said, Don't you dare ask me to do it again.

Mandy didn't.

They had lunch at a hot-dog stand and walked uptown to Times Square.

Mandy filmed the crowds and the lit-up marquees for all the big Broadway shows. "I want to see a Broadway play while I'm here," she said. "But they're so expensive."

Maya showed her the ticket booth at 47th Street and explained that if you stood in line on the day you wanted to go to a show, you could usually get half-price tickets.

"Let's do it tonight!" exclaimed Mandy. "All of us."

"I can't," Maya said. The disappointment showed in her voice.

"I can't, either," said Joy, relieved that she couldn't. She was already sick of Mandy. Besides, she thought, half-price Broadway show tickets still cost plenty.

"We can't, either," Carolyn reminded Mandy. "My dad's taking us out for Chinese food tonight."

"Great!" Mandy exclaimed. "I did a virtual tour of Chinatown on the Internet. I'm dying to go there for real."

"Actually, the Chinese restaurant we're going to is in my neighborhood," Carolyn explained as she held Mandy back from crossing the street against the light. A taxi zoomed by, right where Mandy would have stepped, but she didn't seem to notice.

Maya looked up at a digital clock high above Times Square. "I have to go, you guys," she announced, "I have to pick up my sisters."

Joy watched Maya and Mandy hug good-bye and thought, Mandy already likes Maya better than she likes me. Everybody loves Maya.

The remaining three girls continued "Day One of Mandy's Trip" by walking east on 42nd Street toward Fifth Avenue and then walking north. Their first big stop was St. Patrick's Cathedral. Mandy filmed it from the outside.

Inside, stained-glass windows cast rays of colored light. Huge columns reached upward far above them to meet arches. There were stands of candles dotted throughout the space. Carolyn headed toward one to light a candle in memory of her mother. As she picked up a taper, she noticed that Mandy was filming her. "This will be perfect for the movie," she whispered.

"Don't film me in here," Carolyn blurted out in a loud voice.

A woman lighting a candle at the same stand scowled at her.

Carolyn whispered, "Sorry," to the woman and put the taper back without lighting a candle.

Mandy had turned to Joy. "Do you have someone you could light a candle for?"

"No," answered Joy. No way was she bringing Uncle Brett into Mandy's video.

Mandy went over to the woman who'd hushed Carolyn. While she talked to her, Carolyn walked down the center aisle of the cathedral. I wanted to light a candle for you, Mom, she thought. But not for a video. I miss you so much. I don't understand Mandy anymore. It's like she's a stranger.

Carolyn spotted another stand of candles tucked in behind a column. Looking over her shoulder, she saw that Mandy was busy taping the woman lighting a candle. She ducked around the column, put a dollar in the contribution slot, and lit a candle. When she turned she saw Joy, sitting in a pew watching her. She sat next to her.

"I'm tired of walking," admitted Joy.

"Me, too," agreed Carolyn. "But it's fun to see

everything." She looked around at the vast spaces of the cathedral. "I've never been here before."

Next they visited — and Mandy'd taped — Rockefeller Center, Radio City Music Hall, rush hour traffic, and the glitzy Plaza Hotel. When they left the Plaza, Joy announced, "I 'm not walking another step."

"We just have one more place to check out," said Mandy. "FAO Schwarz. It's right across the street."

On the first floor of the big toy store, they checked out stuffed animals and puppets. Mandy had Carolyn take her picture with a life-sized stuffed giraffe. They took an elevator that looked like a Transformer toy to the second floor. Joy saw at least a dozen things she would have liked to buy for her brother but couldn't afford.

They were checking out a display of vintage Barbie and Ken dolls when Carolyn said, "We have to go home soon. I told my dad we'd be there by six-thirty."

Mandy turned away from Barbie and Ken in a pink convertible with their surfboards to face Carolyn. "Let's call and say we'll be there at seven-thirty. There's this place I want to check out first. You should come, too, Joy."

"What place?" asked Carolyn.

"Do we have to walk there?" added Joy.

Mandy pulled a business card out of her pants pocket. "It's called Mais Oui and it's on west Twenty-first Street and Tenth Avenue. That neighborhood is called Chelsea, right?"

"Right," agreed Carolyn.

"I've eaten at Mais Oui," commented Joy. "With my dad. How come you want to go?" She thought but didn't add, Mais Oui is really expensive.

Mandy smiled. "A guy I know works there." She winked at Carolyn. "I told him I'd stop by and say hi."

"The guy from the plane?" asked Carolyn.

Mandy answered with a nod. "Can I borrow your phone?" she asked Joy.

"Carolyn's number is four on speed dial," Joy said as she handed over the phone.

"Don't tell him it's because you want to see Airplane Guy," Carolyn warned Mandy.

Mandy gave her a look that said, *I'm smarter than that,* then spoke into the phone, "Hi, Dr. Kuhlberg. It's me, Mandy . . ."

A minute later they had permission. They said good-bye to Barbie and Ken and left the toy store to take the E train to Chelsea.

Mais Oui

After Maya finished babysitting her sisters she went outside to try the digital camera. She looked at the LCD screen to line up a shot of the corner market and pushed the button.

Long shot of a man in a bright yellow shirt in front of boxes of colorful fruits and vegetables.

A second passed before she heard the click. She reviewed the shot. The man was almost out of the frame. "Darn," she mumbled.

Joy had told them about the time lag in class. "You get used to it," she'd said. Maya remembered the great shots Joy had taken with her digital camera. Well, if she can do it, she thought, I can, too. She took ten more shots of people in colorful outfits passing the display of produce. She didn't like the first nine pictures. She deleted those and kept the last one.

Woman in brown-and-orange African dress and head wrap walking by crates of green and purple grapes.

Maya switched the camera off and turned it over in her hand. It's smaller and lighter than Grandpa's camera, she thought. Which is good. And I don't have to pay to develop ten shots to find one I like. That's good, too. Maybe digital isn't so bad.

After photographing all that fruit, Maya wanted to eat some. She crossed the street, picked out a bunch of green grapes, and went into the market to buy them.

Mr. Rodriquez was at the register. "How's the Johnson girl today?" he asked as he weighed the grapes.

She paid for the grapes. "I'm good."

As she left the store she thought about the day Mr. Rodriquez thought she was lost. She had been a little kid then. It was Hannah's christening party and no one had had time to take her to the swings. So she decided to go by herself. She'd stopped in front of the pretty fruits and vegetables. Mr. Rodriquez saw her alone, took her by the hand, and brought her inside his store. She sat on the stool next to the ice cream cooler while he called her parents. Right away, her father came in a white-and-blue police car. He and some other officers from the local police precinct were already out looking for her. Everyone thought she'd run away because she was jealous of the baby.

"You'll have your own party for your birthday," her father had promised. Then he scolded her for going out alone. Maya remembered being confused by how everyone was acting — all upset with her and happy she was safe at the same time. But she still didn't get to go to the swings.

When the party finally ended, her grandmother

brought her downstairs for a bath in her apartment. As she helped her into star-and-moon pajamas, she said, "You didn't run away today, did you?"

Maya shook her head no, relieved that someone finally believed her. "I wanted to go to the swings."

Gran had kissed her forehead and said, "I know. Next time ask me to take you."

How can I ever put all of that memory into a photograph? Maya wondered.

Mandy stood under the burgundy awning of an outdoor café. "Just push that red record button," she directed Carolyn. "Like I showed you." Carolyn looked through the lens at Mandy, smiling, and started recording.

Mandy flashed a TV-reporter smile at the camera. "I'm in Chelsea. It's on the West Side of Manhattan, from Fourteenth Street to Thirtieth Street. This neighborhood is an oasis of trendy shops and restaurants. It's a hip place to live." She flashed the smile again.

Joy leaned against a lamppost watching Mandy's performance and thought, This is going to be a stupid video. Mandy is so full of herself she doesn't even know it.

Mandy took back the camera and turned it on Carolyn. "Tell me, what do you like about Chelsea, Carolyn?"

Carolyn blinked in surprise at suddenly being on camera. "There — ah — are a lot of art galleries around here," she managed to stammer. "Some of them show photography. I went to a photography exhibit in this neighborhood. Once." She pointed west toward the river. "And Chelsea Piers is over there. It's a sports complex. They even have horseback riding. But I've never gone there. Just Rollerbladed by it. That's all I know." She forced a smile at the camera. She knew that she'd sounded really lame.

A bike messenger who'd stopped for a light was watching the interview.

Mandy slowly panned the camera to the messenger. "Want to be on TV?"

"Sure," he answered, "if you make it fast."

"I'm not letting her shoot me anymore," Joy whispered to Carolyn.

"Me, either," agreed Carolyn. "It's kind of embarrassing. Especially when she doesn't warn you."

The first thing Carolyn noticed when they walked into Mais Oui was that it was fancier than any restaurant she'd ever been in. The walls were painted a soft yellow and trimmed with fancy white woodwork. The tables were covered with white tablecloths, candles, and fresh flowers. Waiters in burgundy jackets moved gracefully around the room. Classical music was playing in the background.

A maître d' greeted them with, "*Bonjour, mademoiselles.* Have you a reservation?"

"*Bonjour,*" Mandy answered.

Carolyn looked at Mandy, surprised.

"*Je désire parler avec mon ami, Paul*," Mandy continued in halting French.

Joy was embarrassed by Mandy's stiff sounding schoolgirl French. Except for saying "bonjour" instead of "hello," the maître d' had spoken to them in English. Mandy should have just said, "I'd like to speak to my friend, Paul."

The maître d' nodded in the direction of the bar and said slowly and clearly, to be sure that she would understand. "*Paul est là*."

Carolyn turned. Airplane Guy was behind the bar. A huge arrangement of orange, purple, and yellow tropical flowers stood guard at the edge of a shiny copper bar. A small group of customers was at the other end, chatting in hushed voices.

"*Merci beaucoup*," Mandy said cheerfully before heading to the bar. Carolyn and Joy followed her.

Paul looked surprised to see Mandy there, but he greeted her courteously. He took in Joy and Carolyn with a smiling glance. "How's your trip been so far?"

Carolyn checked out the people at the end of the bar. The men were dressed in suits and the woman had on a gray suit with a shortish skirt and pointy shoes. Her black hair was pulled back tight. The woman suddenly turned toward Carolyn. Embarrassed to be dressed in jeans, she looked down at her sneakers. She had a flashback of meeting Maxine Geng at a big party at the Museum of Natural History.

M. G.'s black hair was pulled back like that. And she seemed sort of snobby, too. Carolyn glanced up. The woman was still looking their way, but it wasn't M. G.

Mandy was telling Paul all the things she'd done on her first day in New York. "I can't serve you girls at the bar," he said, interrupting her. "Even nonalcoholic drinks. If you want to eat —"

"We just stopped by to say hi," Mandy explained.

Paul's attention had shifted from Mandy to a waiter signaling him from the other end of the bar. As he brought the waiter the two drinks he'd been mixing, Mandy took out her camera and turned it on. She aimed it at Paul and the people standing at the bar.

Joy was about to tell Mandy that she shouldn't shoot in the restaurant when Paul saw the camera. He motioned Mandy to stop and hurried back to them. "You can't tape in here," he said in a low firm voice.

"Sorry," Mandy said as she put the camera away.

The tight-haired woman was now heading toward them. Joy thought that she looked like the woman Carolyn's father dated. But it wasn't her.

The woman stopped in front of Joy and asked, "Aren't you Ted Cohen's daughter?"

"Yes," answered Joy, now sure it wasn't Dr. Kuhlberg's old girlfriend. But the woman did look familiar.

"I met you at the office," the woman continued. "Your father and I worked together. How is Ted doing? We all felt —"

"He's okay," Joy said, cutting the woman off. She didn't want this woman talking about her father being fired in front of Carolyn and Mandy. "He's really busy." She smiled at the woman and grabbed Carolyn's arm. "We have to go. Nice to see you."

"Tell your father that Michelle says hello. We miss him."

"I will," agreed Joy. "Thanks. Bye."

Joy steered Carolyn toward the exit, leaving Mandy still talking to Airplane Guy.

The maître d' opened the door for them. "*Au revoir, monsieur,*" Carolyn said as she passed him.

The moment they were outside, Carolyn burst out laughing.

"What's so funny?" asked Joy.

"Talking French," Carolyn said. "And that woman. First, I thought she was M. G. Then I thought she was upset that we were there. You know, because we're dressed like this. Then she knew you. And Airplane Guy is like ten years older than us. And —"

A grin broke across Joy's face. "I thought she looked like M. G., too."

"You did?" Carolyn was about to tell Joy how M. G. and her father were still friends and that she was afraid they'd start dating again when she realized that Mandy was shooting.

Joy saw, too. She put up her hand to block Mandy's view of her. "Enough," she said sternly.

"Okay," Mandy agreed, turning off the camera.

Carolyn looked from Mandy to Joy. Joy, she could see, was angry with Mandy. But Mandy didn't even seem to notice. She was still in Cheerful Tourist mode.

"You shouldn't just shoot without warning," Carolyn whispered.

Mandy nodded that she understood, but Carolyn wasn't so sure that she did.

As they walked away from the restaurant, Mandy walked between Joy and Carolyn and linked arms. "Mais Oui is a lousy name for that restaurant."

"Why?" asked Carolyn.

"'Mais oui' means 'but yes.' Everything in there was 'but no.' No, you can't sit at the bar. No, I can't serve you. No, you can't shoot in here. Paul should find a friendlier place to work."

Joy smiled despite herself. "You have a point."

When Maya's subway pulled into the 79th Street station the next morning, Carolyn and Mandy got on. Maya made room for them at the center pole before the train jerked out of the station.

"What'd you guys do after I left yesterday?" she asked. "Did you have fun?"

"We did," Mandy answered enthusiastically. "I shot a lot. I can play it for you."

At the next stop, Maya spotted three seats and pulled Mandy to sit next to her. "Show me."

Mandy took the camera and the attached headphones out of her orange messenger bag. Maya put on the headset, pressed PLAY, and watched the footage in the LCD display. Carolyn leaned against Maya's shoulder so she could see, too.

Images of Times Square, Fifth Avenue, and St. Patrick's Cathedral moved across the small screen. The footage of Chelsea finished as the train pulled into the 42nd Street station and it was time to change trains.

"So far, I love your video," Maya told Mandy. They were walking through the tunnel to the N and R trains. "I think they'll air it."

"If you cut out the part where I sound so stupid," Carolyn put in.

Mandy turned to her. "I thought you were great in that scene."

"I like that candid-camera quality," agreed Maya. "It's more like real life."

Real life isn't someone sticking a camera in your face without warning, thought Carolyn.

Maya was leading the way out of the Eighth Street station when they met Serge on the platform. Maya handed him her paper.

Mandy put out her hand to shake with Serge. "You must be Serge. I'm Mandy."

"You are friend of Carolyn from Why-o-min," Serge said in his sweet, formal way. "I am very happy to meet you, Mandy,"

Mandy held up the camera. "Can I film you, Serge? I'd like you to be a character in this film I'm making about New York City."

"I am going to my English class now," Serge answered. Maya heard disappointment in his voice.

"Can I shoot you getting on the subway?" asked Mandy.

Carolyn could see over Mandy's shoulder that she already had the camera turned on.

"I will be big American movie star," Serge said happily. A train pulled into the station. "But I have to go now."

"I'll shoot you getting on the train," Mandy offered. She followed Serge with the camera as he ran toward the opening doors. Before he stepped in, he turned, waved good-bye, and shouted, "See you later, alligator."

Carolyn and Maya exchanged a grin. "Maybe his English teacher's like sixty years old or something," Carolyn commented.

Mandy ran up to them. "Serge is cute. 'See you later, alligator' is so old-fashioned."

Carolyn, happy that she and Mandy had the same thought, put an arm around Mandy's shoulder. "That's what we just said."

Joy was disappointed to see Mandy walk into the workshop with Carolyn and Maya.

Carolyn introduced Mandy to Beth and the members of the workshop.

"Are you just here for the day, Mandy?" Beth asked. "To observe?"

Mandy held up her video camera. "I'd like to participate. It's digital."

"You know how to use that?" asked Ousmane.

Mandy told them all about the video production class she'd taken, how the public-access station had lent her the camera, and that she was shooting in New York City. She even told them about Mandrina Productions.

Beth, Ousmane, and Janice asked her a lot of questions.

Mandy's taking over the whole class, Joy thought. She's so pushy.

Maya was thinking, Mandy has so much energy and self-confidence. I wish I could be like that.

Carolyn, remembering how quiet Mandy used to be in school, wondered how a person could change so much.

Beth smiled at Mandy. "Thank you for all that. You already know a lot about video."

I hate know-it-alls, thought Joy.

Next, Beth asked for volunteers to describe their first experiences with the digital camera and show the pictures they took on the computer monitor. Carolyn didn't volunteer to talk about her experiences with the camera because she didn't have any. Mandy's tour was taking up all her time.

At the end of the session, Beth reminded the class that, for anyone who hadn't paid yet, the fee for the workshop was now overdue. Joy turned her attention to her fingers so she wouldn't have to meet Beth's gaze.

"See you Tuesday," Beth said as she dismissed them. "Use those cameras."

Carolyn turned to Joy and asked, "Are you coming with us?" Mandy, she could see out of the corner of her eye, was talking to Ousmane.

Joy pushed out her chair and stood. "Where does Mandy want to go today?"

"Statue of Liberty and Ground Zero for starters. But that's okay. I've never been to the Statue of Liberty, so I'm kind of into that part. Can you come?"

"I'm babysitting," Joy answered even though she wasn't. Today she had to go to her dad's to pack up the stuff that was in her room. The move was the next day.

Maya had joined them. "I can't go, either, CK. I'm working at the store. But don't forget you're all invited to a sleepover at my house tomorrow night. Jay-Cee's coming."

"What about Shana?" Carolyn asked, hoping that Shana couldn't come. She was sure that Shana wouldn't like Mandy.

Maya thought the same thing. Mandy and her in-your-face camera style would not sit well with Shana.

"I didn't invite her," admitted Maya.

Good, thought Carolyn.

Mandy ran up to them. "Guess what, you guys?" she said excitedly. "Ousmane invited us all to his restaurant. It's in Brooklyn. And I'll shoot there. Maybe I can interview his family. They all work in the restaurant. He was born in Senegal in West Africa. They've only been here, like, ten years. It's a real immigrant story for my video. And he's Muslim. He said there are a lot of Muslims in New York."

Carolyn thought, Mandy just asked him all this stuff about his life. She's become the total opposite of shy.

"Don't forget about the sleepover at my house tomorrow," Maya reminded Mandy.

"Perfect," Mandy said as she waved good-bye to Ousmane. "We can all go to Brooklyn together after we get up and have some of your famous pancakes."

Mandy and Maya started talking about Brooklyn and walked out together. Carolyn and Joy followed. "How'd she know about the pancakes?" asked Joy.

"I guess I told her," answered Carolyn. "We used to e-mail a lot."

Maybe I told Mandy too much, Carolyn thought. How can she remember all these details? I hardly remember anything about what she told me in e-mails a year ago.

When they were on the street, Mandy waited for Joy. "You have to come with us today. To the Statue of Liberty and Ground Zero."

"She's babysitting," Carolyn said. "Maya can't come, either."

"I'm really sorry I can't," Maya said. Carolyn could tell she was sincere.

"But you *have* to come to Ground Zero with us, Joy," Mandy pleaded. "That's where I want to interview you about when you saw the towers fall."

Joy shot an angry look at Carolyn. Why'd she tell Mandy that?

Carolyn mouthed, "Sorry." And she was. Why

did Mandy have to blab everything she ever told her to Joy and Maya? It was like she was bragging about knowing so much about their lives.

"Carolyn told you I can't go, Mandy," Joy was saying. "Didn't you hear her? I'm babysitting." Besides, thought Joy, I don't talk about what I saw on 9/11. I don't want to remember. It's too upsetting. I especially would never, ever tell *you* about it.

"You can bring your baby brother, Joy," Mandy said. "That'll be a nice touch."

"You're not putting my brother in your stupid video," shouted Joy. "Or me." She hitched her bag over her shoulder and walked away. She imagined Jake in his little stroller at Ground Zero, watching and listening to her talk about the most horrible thing she'd ever seen. Even if he didn't understand the words, he would be able to tell that she was upset. He had enough upsetting things going on in his little life already. Tears stung her eyes.

Maya saw Mandy's dimpled smile shrink into a worried look. "What's her problem?"

Right now, you're her problem, thought Carolyn.

"Joy doesn't like to talk about 9/11," explained Maya. "But don't worry, she won't stay mad."

Yes, she will, thought Carolyn. Joy hates Mandy and that's that.

Atlantic Avenue

Friday, Joy went downtown to help her father and Sue with the move. A moving van was already out front. No more bedroom for me at Dad's, she thought as she went into the building. Her father was in the hallway holding Jake on his hip and giving directions to a mover. Two other movers walked out of the apartment with the couch.

Jake stretched his arms toward his sister. "Oy, Oy."

Her father handed Jake over and said, "Sue could use your help in the kitchen."

Joy held Jake close. "So you're moving today, Jakey," she murmured into his warm cheek.

Sue was standing in front of the open refrigerator. "I totally forgot to pack this stuff!" she wailed. "I am so sick of packing. I told your father he should hire movers who would pack everything for us."

Jake's little body stiffened. Like it does before he cries, Joy thought. She hoisted him above her head and grinned up at him. "Hey, Jakey, how about we go for a walk to the swings?"

"I was going to ask you to empty the refrigerator for me," whined Sue. "I hate food!"

All you talk about is food, thought Joy. And how many calories everything is. And your weight. "I think it's better for Jake to go out," Joy said. "Moving is hard on a kid."

Sue pulled a bottle of water out of the refrigerator and opened it. "Your father said I have to stop buying bottled water. That New York City water is, like, the best in the world." She made an effort to smile at Joy, but it looked more like a grimace. "Go ahead and take Jake out. We should be at the new place in a couple of hours. I'll call you when we're there. Do you have your cell phone?"

Joy nodded.

Before taking Jake out, she went to her bedroom for one last time. It had been her room for seven years. She stood at the window. "I remember the first time I looked out this window," she told Jake, even though he was too young to understand.

She was just a little kid herself then, but older than Jake. She'd felt awful about the divorce — scared, sad, and angry all at the same time. The first night she spent at her dad's new apartment, he showed her the view from her window. The World Trade Center loomed ahead of them in the orangey-pink glow of sunset. Her father had put an arm around her and said that he loved her and that everything would be all right. After dinner that night she went back to the window and looked out again. Lights sparkled up and down the 110-story buildings. "Good night, Twin Towers," she had whispered. Every morning and night that she was at her dad's, she started and ended the day by looking at the Twin Towers. That's what she was doing the day they fell.

Jake pulled on her sleeve. "Out."

She gave him a little hug. "Out! You know a new word, Jakey." She turned from the window. "So let's go out."

Carolyn let Mandy shoot her going into Maya's mother's store, Remember Me. Mrs. Johnson was up front with a customer. "Maya's in the workroom," she called to Carolyn. "You can go on back."

Mandy stopped to flip through a rack of satin jackets. "This place is fabulous." She pulled out a hot pink one that read BAYSIDE ROLLER RINK. She was wearing the jacket when they went into the storeroom. Jay-Cee was at the sewing machine. Maya was steaming wrinkles out of a red lace gown.

Maya pointed the steamer at Mandy. "Great jacket on you."

Jay-Cee looked up. "Hey, hi. You must be Mandy. I'm Jay-Cee."

"Hi," Mandy returned. She held up her camera. "Can I film you guys in here?"

"As long as I get to plug my Jay-Cee Originals line of clothing," Jay-Cee answered.

Carolyn stood behind a rack of still-wrinkled clothes so she wouldn't be in the shot.

Mandy filmed the crammed room, stopping on Jay-Cee. "Tell me all about Jay-Cee Originals."

Carolyn wasn't surprised that Jay-Cee didn't mind having the video camera in her face. She planned on paying for college by modeling and loved to have her picture taken.

After the taping, they went out into the shop and tried on clothes.

Jay-Cee and Maya picked out clothes for Mandy to try on and helped her decide what to get. She bought a pair of black-and-gray–checked capri pants, a denim miniskirt, the hot pink satin jacket, and a Jay-Cee Originals blue halter for herself and a red one for Katrina back home.

"Of course I've given you the ten percent friends-of-Maya discount," Mrs. Johnson said as she folded the merchandise. She smiled at Carolyn. "Nothing for you today?"

Carolyn put a light-green Jay-Cee Originals halter on the counter.

Maya gave a little tug to a lock of Carolyn's red hair. "To go with her hair."

"Her mother always bought her green clothes," observed Mandy. "She was great. Everyone loved Carolyn's mother. I still miss her." She turned to Carolyn. "Don't you just miss her something awful?"

Maya knew talking about her mother made Carolyn sad. Mandy clearly didn't know it. "She's told us about her," she answered for Carolyn. "Listen, you guys, we have to get back to my house. Joy's meeting us there."

*   *   *

When Joy finally left her father's new apartment, Jake was asleep in his crib and her father and Sue were arguing about why Sue threw out the stuff in their old refrigerator instead of packing it. On the train uptown to Maya's, Joy worried that Jake would wake up and hear them. By the time she reached Harlem, she realized that her father hadn't paid her for babysitting. Did he think he didn't have to pay her because it was moving day? she wondered.

Maya's younger sister, Hannah, greeted Joy at the front door to the Johnson house. "I'm braiding hair for Maya's sleepover." She checked the small pad in her hand. "I could fit you in at eight o'clock." Looking up, she added, "Carolyn already made her appointment."

Joy ran her hand through her own short black hair. She'd look silly with braids. "Maybe another time, Hannah."

Laughter tumbled down the stairwell from Maya's room two floors above.

When Joy came into Maya's room, Jay-Cee exclaimed, "Hey, Joy. Where you been?"

"Babysitting," Joy answered as she looked around to make sure Mandy wasn't shooting her again.

She wasn't. Mandy was sitting cross-legged in the middle of the bed looking through an album of photographs that Maya had taken in the photo class.

"What are you going to do for the workshop?" Joy asked Maya. "Did you decide?"

"Something about being a kid. You know, a memory from childhood, I think. Beth wants us to use Photoshop, and I'll definitely need it for that. What about you?"

"No idea."

"Me, neither," admitted Carolyn. "I haven't even tried using the camera yet."

No one said anything for a minute. Mandy continued going through the album. Carolyn was sitting on the floor flipping through a fashion magazine with Jay-Cee, and Maya was looking at her photo album over Mandy's shoulder.

They aren't laughing anymore, Joy noticed. Did I do that? Am I such a downer? She sat on the edge of the bed next to Maya. "What were you guys laughing about a minute ago?" she asked. "I heard you all the way downstairs."

"Carolyn was telling us about going to that French restaurant. She did a great imitation of the woman she thought was M. G."

Joy saw that Carolyn's hair was pulled back in a tight bun like the woman. She poked Carolyn with her foot. "You got the hair right. Do it for me."

Carolyn stood up and pulled herself into a stiff posture. She pursed her lips and asked in a clipped, businesslike voice, "Aren't you Ted Cohen's daughter?"

Joy laughed. "Very good," she said. "That is funny."

"M. G. doesn't sound like any fun, though," commented Jay-Cee. "I'm glad someone stiff like that isn't dating your dad anymore."

"Dr. K can be pretty uptight himself," commented Mandy. She looked up at Carolyn. "No offense."

"I know," agreed Carolyn. It didn't upset her to talk about her dad like that. Everyone knew he was a formal kind of guy. She just hoped Mandy wouldn't start talking about her mother again.

"But your dad's worse since your mom died." Mandy added. "You have to admit that."

"What was she like, CK?" Jay-Cee asked.

Maya saw Carolyn's pale skin fade to paler. Time to change the subject. "Hey, let's order pizza." She pointed a finger at Jay-Cee. "I should warn you all that *she* is going to want pineapple on it."

"I love pineapple on my pizza, too!" exclaimed Mandy.

Hannah came to the doorway. "It's time for your appointment, Carolyn," she announced in a voice as businesslike as the woman at Mais Oui. "Would you like me to do it here or in my room — I mean, my *salon*?"

They all cracked up.

While they waited for the pizza, Hannah braided Carolyn's hair.

After they finished eating, they all changed into boxer shorts and T-shirts. Carolyn looked around. Mandy's makeup had worn off, and in shorts and a T she looked more like her old self. Everyone seemed to be having a good time. Joy, too. Maybe having Mandy visit for two weeks would be okay.

Hannah came back from her own dinner to

braid Mandy's hair. When she left, the subject went back to Carolyn's father's love life.

"He should be with someone who is different from him," observed Mandy. "His wife was very different, and they got along great."

Maya shot Carolyn a sympathetic glance. But Carolyn didn't notice because she was looking down at the straw she was nervously tying into knots.

"Someone full of life," Mandy continued, "who'd loosen him up a little."

"Someone like Ivy," suggested Jay-Cee. "That'd be great for you, too, Carolyn. Imagine having Ivy for a stepmother."

I do like Ivy a lot, thought Carolyn. But I can't imagine Dad and her as a couple.

"I don't think they'd like each other. They don't have anything in common," observed Joy.

"You can't know that for sure," protested Mandy. "Don't be so negative."

Joy glared in Mandy's direction.

"Ivy might already have a boyfriend," said Maya, glad that they'd at least gotten off the subject of Carolyn's mother.

Mandy put up a finger. "That is the first thing we have to figure out. Carolyn, you and I will check it out Monday morning when we walk the dogs with her. And if Ivy doesn't have a boyfriend already, do you know what we have to do next?"

"What?" asked Maya and Jay-Cee in unison.

"We have to put Ivy and Dr. K in the same place at the same time."

"That free concert she's in!" shouted Maya. "That'd be perfect. There's a party afterward and everything."

"Remember when he brought us all to Saint John the Divine for that concert?" added Joy, getting into the spirit. "Ivy played that night,"

"He thought she was good," Maya said, continuing the thought. "He said something like" — Maya lowered her voice to sound like Dr. K — "'I'm surprised that she is such a serious musician.'"

"My friends," announced Mandy, "we have a plan for Operation Romance."

This is never going to work, thought Carolyn. Not in a million years. My dad and Ivy? No way.

The next morning, Mandy insisted on making pancakes for the sleepover guests and for Maya's little sisters. Naomi looked down at the three perfect heart-shaped pancakes Mandy had put on her plate. "Joy makes crooked heart ones," she observed.

"Mandy scores again," Joy mumbled to Carolyn.

"She always made good pancakes," whispered Carolyn. "But I didn't know she could make them in shapes." Is that something else Mandy learned from Katrina? she wondered.

After breakfast Jay-Cee went to Remember Me to sew up more halter tops. The remaining four girls walked around Harlem for a couple of hours so Mandy could shoot the neighborhood. Then they took the train to Brooklyn.

When they came out of the subway, Mandy told Carolyn, "I can't wait to tell Katrina about the sleepover."

"She'll see the video," Carolyn reminded her.

Joy led the way through Brooklyn Heights. They stood on the promenade overlooking the East River toward Manhattan. The Brooklyn Bridge hung across the river to their right. From the promenade they walked down to the Fulton Street Mall, where carless streets were lined with stores and thick with foot traffic.

"The restaurant should be near here," Maya announced when they'd walked away from the mall. "I'll go down the next street and look."

Carolyn and Joy stayed on the corner and watched Mandy taping a street performer juggling tennis balls.

Joy leaned toward Carolyn and asked, "Are you having a good time with Mandy?"

"I guess. But whenever we're alone, she's either talking on the phone to Katrina or e-mailing her. When she's not doing that, she's talking about her video."

Maya was back. "I found it."

Ousmane was waiting for them at the door to Dakar West.

As Carolyn walked in, the odor of cooking

spices surrounded her and triggered her taste buds. Her mouth watered. "It smells so good," she commented to Ousmane.

"My father's the chef," Ousmane said. A girl with dark hair and even darker eyes came out from the back of the restaurant. "This is my sister, Fatou."

Fatou and Ousmane could talk for only a few minutes before they had to go back to serving food to the other customers. The girls sat at a table near the back of the restaurant.

Maya looked around at the bright-colored fabrics hanging on the walls. They reminded her of the long dress — a bubu — and head-tie that West African women in her neighborhood wore. Her grandmother had an aqua-and-black bubu that she'd bought on her trip to West Africa.

Ousmane served them barbecued lemon chicken and onions over rice. After they'd finished that, Fatou brought them a green salad with chopped eggs and French bread.

"It's all delicious," commented Mandy. "Do you have time to sit with us?"

Fatou shook her head. "I'm helping prepare food for tonight. We're very busy on Saturday nights. But I'm glad you came."

"Is Hoyt Street near here?" asked Maya.

"Just a couple of blocks," she answered.

"Why do you want to know?" Mandy wondered.

"A friend of mine lives there," answered Maya.

Shana, thought Carolyn.

Maya leaned toward Joy. "Can I borrow your phone?"

Joy handed her the phone and Maya went out front to make her call. Shana's probably not there, Maya thought as she waited for someone to pick up on the other end. She's probably doing something with Alex.

"Hello." It was Shana!

"Hi, it's me. Maya. Guess where I am?"

"You're calling on a cell from a noisy street," answered Shana. "You're on 125th?"

"No," answered Maya, happy that Shana was home, happy to hear her voice. "I'm on Atlantic Avenue." She looked at the sign for the cross street. "And Nevins Street."

"That's, like, around the corner from me. What are you doing there?"

Shana's really glad that I'm here, thought Maya. I'll go over to her aunt's house. The others can go back to Manhattan alone or just hang out in Brooklyn some more if they want. And I can hang out with Shana.

"There's this African restaurant. Dakar West. A new guy in our workshop, his family owns it. We just ate there."

"I know that place," Shana said. "I'll come on over. Wait for me."

Maya was about to say she'd go to Shana's, but it was too late. Shana had already hung up. She went back into the restaurant and gave the phone back to

Joy. "Shana lives near here. She's going to drop by. Then I'm going to go hang out with her for a while. Okay?"

"Shana!" exclaimed Mandy. "The one who writes all that cool poetry."

Maya nodded. "I haven't seen Shana since she moved to Brooklyn."

Mandy knows all about Shana, thought Carolyn, because I'm such a blabbermouth.

Mandy held up her camera. "I can't wait to meet her. I'll tape her doing her poetry."

Maya remembered how angry Shana got when she'd photographed her at the slam poetry contest. "I'm not so sure she'll like that," she told Mandy.

Let Mandy try, thought Joy. Shana is queen of the evil looks. Maybe Shana will finally slow down peppy, in-your-face-with-my-camera Tourist Girl.

Metropolitan Museum of Art

Carolyn saw Shana through the restaurant window. She had on a loose pair of jeans and a red sleeveless T, and her black hair was done up in cornrows that hung down to her shoulders. Carolyn touched the dozens of braids that Hannah had put in her hair. Will Shana give me a hard time about having braids? she wondered. Will she criticize me for copying a black hairstyle? She pulled the braids back and tied them in a knot at the nape of her neck.

As Shana walked in, Ousmane came out from the kitchen with a sampling of desserts. Maya introduced Shana to Ousmane and Mandy.

Mandy reached up and shook Shana's hand. "I'm really glad to meet you. I heard all about how you perform your own poetry."

Shana sat down. "I don't know how great my poems are," she said in a friendly enough voice. "But thanks, anyway. Hey, how's your trip to New York going? You having fun?"

Carolyn and Joy exchanged a surprised glance. Shana was actually being nice to a new friend of Maya's?

While they ate dessert, Mandy asked Shana how the slam competition worked. Then Mandy told Shana about the video she was making. "I'd love you to recite one of your poems for my film," Mandy said.

Shana is going to cut her down now, thought Joy. But Shana smiled at Mandy. "Sure. Any publicity is good publicity."

"That's what Jay-Cee said," Mandy told her.

Shana grinned. "I just have to figure out which poem to do."

"Do the one you did at the Apollo," suggested Carolyn. "That was great."

Shana whipped around to face her. "You got braids in your hair, Red."

Here it comes, thought Joy. Shana loves to put down Carolyn. I've got to step in and help her out here. But before Joy could, Carolyn spoke up for herself. "Hannah braided my hair. I paid her."

Shana softened. "Hannah did those braids? Good for her. You know, Red, they'd look better if you just left them loose."

"Maybe," Carolyn shot back, but she didn't untie the knot of braids.

Joy gave Carolyn a pat on the back.

"Can I tape Shana here?" Mandy asked Ousmane.

"Sure," he answered. "We have live entertainment at Dakar West sometimes." He looked around the restaurant. "Besides, you're the only ones here now."

Shana smiled at Mandy. "Where do you want me?"

Mandy pointed her camera at a person-sized plant near the front window. "Over there."

Shana and Mandy went to the front to set up. A few minutes later, she performed a poem that Carolyn hadn't heard before, "Free Me."

I came from you and lived with you
But that doesn't mean you own me.

You call me bad And make me sad
But that doesn't make you right.

Angry words and acts explode from you
What am I supposed to do?
Accept every blow?
I don't think so.

Your mental pains are chains that hold me
   tight,
Keep me from the light.
But those chains are in your mind,
Not mine.

I have to keep my own goals in sight
And do what I think is right.
So when I walk through any door
I can soar And be me

Free.

Maya knew the poem was about Shana and her mother. Her mother was in a mental hospital now. It bothered Maya that Shana never talked to her about the problems she had at home.

Everyone was applauding — including Ousmane's sister and mother, who'd come out from the kitchen to listen.

Joy loved the dramatic way that Shana performed her poem, using her hands, sometimes speaking loudly, other times — like when she said, "Those chains are in your mind" — in a harsh whisper.

Mandy switched off the camera, then hugged Shana and whispered something in her ear. Carolyn thought she saw tears in Mandy's eyes when she turned around.

Maya thought, I hope I get a chance to be alone with Shana today. I'll ask her how her mom is doing in the hospital. Maybe I'll get to see her aunt's apartment. Maybe she'll even invite me for a sleepover.

"Can I do another poem?" Shana asked Mandy. "Something more upbeat." She looked around at her audience. "It's about Brooklyn."

The Brooklyn poem was funny, fast, and smart. Carolyn liked the part about the different nationalities that lived in Brooklyn. Joy thought the section on different ethnic foods was the best and funniest.

When the poem ended, Shana made a deep bow and Mandy switched off her camera. Maya got up to go over to Shana. Maybe now I can leave with her, she thought.

But before Maya reached Shana, she announced, "I have to go, you guys. I have a slam rehearsal with my team." She thanked Ousmane for the food, made a little wave in Carolyn and Joy's direction, hugged Mandy one more time, and left.

Shana didn't even say good-bye to me, Maya thought as she went back to the table. Carolyn elbowed her. "Shana's trying to get your attention."

Maya looked up. Shana was pointing in her direction and holding her hand like a telephone with the thumb pointing to her ear and little finger to her mouth. She wants me to call her, thought Maya. Maybe then we can make plans to do something together, just the two of us.

Mandy interrupted her thoughts. "Maya, I need Shana's phone number. She wants me to call her."

The next morning, Mandy and Carolyn walked across Central Park to meet Maya and Joy at the Metropolitan Museum of Art.

"It's huge!" Mandy exclaimed as she took out her video camera.

Carolyn pointed to the wide front stairs studded with museum-goers. "Look. There's Joy and Maya. That's Joy in the bright yellow top."

Mandy sighted Joy and Maya with the video camera and zoomed in.

"I wouldn't shoot her without asking first," Carolyn reminded her.

Mandy lowered her camera. "You're right. She

can be so grumpy. If I lived here, I'm not so sure I'd want to be Joy's friend."

If you lived here, I don't know if I'd be your friend, Carolyn thought as they headed toward Joy and Maya. *I don't even recognize you anymore. You're so selfish. All you think about is what you want to do. You're taking over my room. You're taking over my life. And, if you could, I bet you'd take over my friends. Except, I guess, you wouldn't want Joy.*

Carolyn was surprised at how angry she felt toward Mandy and so distracted that she bumped into a woman dressed in silver with silver-painted skin. Carolyn let out a little shriek. Silver Woman — a street performer — remained perfectly still and didn't even look to see who'd bumped into her. A few people clapped, as if Carolyn were part of the act. She went over to Joy and Maya and sat between them on the steps.

"Good going, CK," teased Joy.

"Watch her," Maya whispered to Carolyn. "She's so still. I don't know how she does it."

The woman was being a statue. Mandy shot her and the people on the steps watching. Joy took out her camera and went over to take some still shots. So did Maya.

I'd love to get close-ups of that woman's silver face, thought Carolyn. It might help me get some ideas for my photography project. But in the rush to leave the house, she'd forgotten her camera. She stayed on the steps watching the others take pictures.

The woman slowly, slowly, slowly turned her head. Now she was looking right at Carolyn. Carolyn looked back into her silver-rimmed blue eyes. Even her eyelashes were silver. Not once did those silver eyelids flicker. Carolyn's eyes started to water. She blinked and looked away.

Joy moved to the other end of the steps to photograph a man playing guitar and singing in Spanish.

Carolyn watched the musician for a minute before looking back to Silver Woman. She was still staring in Carolyn's direction, but now her arm was slowly, slowly, slowly moving up. Carolyn smiled to herself and thought, there's always something interesting going on in New York City.

Monday was another hot, humid day. Carolyn walked Precious and Jax along 81st Street toward the park. Mandy had Tyson and Gertrude. Ivy was ahead of them with the remaining three dogs.

Precious, panting from the heat, looked at Carolyn expectantly. She patted his head. "It'll be a little cooler in the park."

Mandy moved closer to Carolyn and whispered, "Ask her."

Ivy turned to them, "Ask me what? Are you expecting a raise so soon, Red?"

"No," said Carolyn, embarrassed. She gave Mandy an I-can't-do-this look.

"We're just wondering if you have a special guy," Mandy explained. "You know, a boyfriend."

"Actually I don't," she said. "Not at the moment. No one special enough, anyway."

"What kind of guys do you like?" asked Mandy.

Ivy looked around at her canine clients. "I'd like a guy version of Precious. Someone smart, quiet, with a great soul. Have you ever noticed that Precious never barks unless he has something important to say?"

Carolyn patted Precious again and thought, a guy like Precious *would* be great.

They'd reached Central Park West and concentrated on getting the dogs across the four lanes of traffic. But as soon as they were in the park, Ivy asked. "What about you girls? What qualities do you look for in a guy?"

Carolyn thought, I want a guy like Precious, too. But he has to like horses. That's very important to me.

"I want a guy who's *cute*," Mandy announced. "Cute is a requirement. And he should love adventure. I want to go around the world with a video camera."

I didn't know that, thought Carolyn. I suppose she's told Katrina all about it.

"So I guess he should be rich," continued Mandy, "to bankroll the trip. Cute, adventurous, and rich. Do you think I can get all that in one guy?"

"Nope!" Ivy laughed.

Mandy seems to get everything she wants, thought Carolyn. So she probably will find a guy just like that.

They all waited while Precious sniffed the grass.

THREE GIRLS IN THE CITY

"Don't you want him to be nice?" Ivy asked Mandy. "And sweet?"

"Oh, yes," she answered. "If he'd be as nice and sweet as Carolyn's dad, that'd be great. Dr. K is one of the nicest people I've ever met. We were thinking of inviting him to your concert. Is that okay?"

"Sure," answered Ivy. "Does he like percussion?"

"He loves it!" Mandy and Carolyn answered in unison.

They grinned at each other. Carolyn remembered how they used to join pinkies and say "Jinx" when they said the same thing at the same time. Mandy had forgotten about stuff like that.

That night, Carolyn's father took Mandy and Carolyn to the Museum of Natural History to see an IMAX movie about the influence of African music on music in the United States. Afterward, they went for ice-cream cones. "I loved that movie," Mandy told Dr. Kuhlberg. "Thanks for taking me. Did you like all the drumming?"

"I most certainly did," he answered. "I spent quite a bit of time in Africa doing research and frequently attended musical events."

Mandy shot a glance at Carolyn before saying, "Carolyn told me that Ivy is a great percussionist."

"I heard her play at the Cathedral of Saint John the Divine. She's a talented young woman."

"She's not so young, Dad," Carolyn said. "She's, like, forty."

Dr. Kuhlberg raised his eyebrows in surprise. "Really?"

"She's playing at a free concert in the park tomorrow night," Mandy said. "With a West African band. You should come with us."

"I might like to do that," Dr. Kuhlberg said. "I'll have to check my calendar."

Carolyn couldn't wait until she and Mandy were alone in her room so they could talk about her father and Ivy and what it would be like for her if they dated. She needed to talk to someone. She wasn't even sure she wanted her father to go out with Ivy. But when the two girls finally were alone, Mandy went online to e-mail Katrina. The angry thoughts Carolyn had about Mandy in front of the museum came flooding back. Even if Mandy did finally want to talk, Carolyn didn't feel like talking to her anymore. Mandy — this new Mandy — wouldn't understand. And she wouldn't care.

The blue light of the computer screen was still flickering when Carolyn drifted off to sleep.

At breakfast the next morning, Mandy asked Dr. Kuhlberg if he was coming with them to the concert.

He looked up from his paper. "I am already committed this evening, Mandy. A colleague called late last night to ask me to look over some research data. I want to help her. But thanks for asking me."

Her? thought Carolyn. "Is it Dr. Geng?" she blurted out.

Her father smiled as if just the thought of Dr.

Geng made him happy. "Yes. Maxine is writing a paper on the cockroach in history."

Mandy, who was standing behind Dr. Kuhlberg, giggled silently. Carolyn looked away from her. The fact that her father was an expert on cockroaches wasn't funny when M. G. was involved.

The two girls met Maya on the subway, third car from the front. Mandy took the seat next to Maya and Carolyn stood in front of them.

"Carolyn's dad isn't coming to the concert," Mandy announced. "But Shana is."

Maya and Carolyn exchanged a surprised look.

"Remember, Maya, you gave me Shana's number?" continued Mandy. "I told her about the concert and she said that, if Alex wanted to, they'd come for sure. Alex sounds like a great guy. I can't wait to meet him. Ousmane's coming, too. And let's invite Serge." She tapped the newspaper on Maya's lap. "We can leave him a note in the paper. The way you always do."

Maya and Mandy wrote a note to Serge on the centerfold of the paper. Carolyn didn't contribute anything. Mandy and Maya didn't need her help.

When they got off at the Eighth Street station, Carolyn spotted Serge. He was hanging out at their regular trash-can meeting spot. Mandy had spotted him, too. She waved the newspaper as she pushed through the crowd.

Maya put an arm around Caroyn's shoulder. "She sort of takes over doesn't she?"

Carolyn smiled a weak smile. "Sort of." She was glad Maya was finally noticing.

By the time they reached Serge he was reading the note. When he finished, he looked up. "I will come. I am working until eight o'clock. I will come after."

"Are you going to your English class now?" asked Mandy.

He nodded.

"I'd love to go with you. Can I?"

"Sure," he answered.

Mandy looked from Maya to Carolyn. "I'll meet you at one o'clock when your workshop is over. At Astor Place." She smiled at Serge. "Will your class let me shoot them?"

"They would be very happy to be in American movie," he said. "I already told my class about you."

A train roared into the station. Carolyn and Maya watched Serge and Mandy run for it.

As the two friends walked toward the media center, Carolyn thought, this is the first time I've been alone with Maya since Mandy came. But Maya's being so quiet. Is she disappointed that Mandy isn't with us? Does she like Mandy better than she likes me?

Maya was thinking about Mandy, too. Does Serge like Mandy more than me? she wondered.

Zeus Tattoo and Piercing

Beth looked around at the workshop participants. "Let's do a little sharing, folks. Have you been thinking about how to represent a dream or memory in photographs?"

"No," Joy answered without thinking.

Jennifer and Ousmane laughed.

Beth arched an eyebrow in Joy's direction. "Really?"

"I have enough trouble with reality," Joy said, trying to explain her outburst.

"Dreams and memories aren't *real*?" asked Beth.

Joy shifted uncomfortably in her seat.

"I have an idea for what I want to do," Maya said to get the attention off Joy. "But I need help with it."

Beth shifted her gaze to Maya. "That's what we're here for."

Joy shot Maya a grateful look.

Maya told them about leaving Hannah's christening party to go to the park when she was three years old and everyone thought she had run away. "For the project I want to use photos of the corner grocery, the swings, and me as a little girl," she explained. "I've already taken pictures of the grocery store. Next, I'll take pictures of swings. I want the swings to look blurry, like they're actually moving." She turned to Joy. "Can I combine all those into one picture in Photoshop?"

"Sure," agreed Joy.

"It might look more like a memory if the old photo of you as a kid is in black and white," suggested Janice.

"My grandfather took loads of black-and-white pictures of me," Maya remembered. "Maybe one of those will work."

Beth looked around at the rest of the group. "So Maya's all set. Who else has an idea?"

Carolyn slipped lower in her seat. All I've done with the digital camera so far is take pictures of Mandy, she thought. And that was only because Mandy asked me to.

Mandy at the Statue of Liberty.

Mandy at Ground Zero.

Mandy in Greenwich Village.

Mandy in the park with Ivy and the dogs.

Mandy in front of the apartment building.

Mandy wanted to include still photos in her movie. "Like the kind tourists take when they're in New York," she'd explained. "It's perfect that you have a digital camera, Carolyn. That makes it easier to edit them into the video."

Perfect for Mandy, thought Carolyn. But what about me? What am I going to do for my project?

Ousmane shot up his hand. "I have an idea. I

want to do a dream — a nightmare, really — of being chased by a gang. I want it to look like a cartoon with those talk bubbles over people's heads. Can you help me put that together in Photoshop, Joy?" he asked.

"Sure," she answered. "It's easy."

Later, as Joy was leaving the workshop with Carolyn and Maya, Beth stopped her. "I haven't received a check from your parents yet," she said. "Would you remind them, please?"

Joy said she would and added, "Sorry." Going up the stairs behind Carolyn and Joy she thought, my mother said, "Get your father to pay for it." And my father said, "It's your mother's turn." So who's going to pay for the workshop?

When the three friends were on the street, Carolyn announced, "Mandy and I ran away once, too."

"I didn't run away," Maya corrected her. "I just went for a walk."

Carolyn laughed. "I believe you."

Joy poked Carolyn in the arm. "Tell us about when you ran away."

"We were six years old," Carolyn began. "Mandy and me. We saddled up our ponies, rolled up our *Little Mermaid* sleeping bags, tied them to the back of our saddles, and loaded our saddlebags with water and food." She smiled at the memory. "Including a couple of carrots for the ponies and a big bag of candy for us."

"You were going to sleep outside?" said Joy. "That's seriously brave. And with horses."

"Well, they were our transportation," explained Carolyn. "And our best friends."

"Why were you running away?" asked Maya.

"Mandy's mother wouldn't let her have a sleep-over at my house."

"Did they find you?" asked Joy. "Or did you just give up and go home?"

Carolyn laughed. "Give up? Me and Mandy? No way. My mom realized that we were missing and followed our trail. She found us a couple hours after we left. Anyway, we weren't lost. I knew *exactly* where we were and how to get back." She spotted Mandy's and Serge's bleached-blond heads from a block away.

"It sounds like fun," Maya said. "Did you get in big trouble?"

Carolyn shook her head. "My mother didn't tell Mandy's mother. But she made us solemnly promise never to run away again."

Mandy and Serge were closer now. Mandy waved and called out, "Take our picture, Carolyn."

Carolyn pulled out her digital camera.

Serge and Mandy, smiling, coming toward the camera. Click.

Mandy close-up. Click.

"Serge and I have a great idea about how to get your father and Ivy together," announced Mandy.

"How?" Maya and Joy asked in unison.

"A party. I'm going to throw a going-away party for myself. To thank everyone for being so nice to me. Especially Dr. K and Ivy." She linked an arm through

Serge's. "We've got it all figured out. We're going to have a picnic in Central Park on Sunday." She smiled at Joy and Maya. "You're invited, too, of course. And Ousmane and Shana."

Carolyn just stared at her, amazed. Mandy's making all these plans without even checking with me.

Mandy's smile had shifted back to Serge. "Serge is going to bring a special Russian dish."

"I will bring pierogies," he explained. "They are small meat pies. My aunt makes them most wonderful."

"Isn't that a great idea for getting Ivy and Dr. K together?" asked Mandy. "It's even better than the concert."

Maya and Carolyn agreed it was a great idea.

"I have a great idea, too," Joy added. "There's a guy around this corner who sells ices."

After the first cold bite of lemon ice, Maya held the paper cone against her forehead. It was another superhot and humid day in the city. "Let's all go for rowboat rides on the lake during the party," she suggested. "We'll try to get Ivy and Dr. K in a boat together. Just the two of them."

"That's *perfect*!" exclaimed Mandy. "I can't wait for my party." Her smile turned into a frown. "Except for one thing. On Sunday I'll only have two more days left in New York." She put an arm around Joy and one around Maya. "I'll miss you guys."

What about me? Carolyn wondered. Won't you miss me? I bet you didn't even miss me when I moved here.

Mandy pulled Maya and Joy closer. "Take our picture," she directed Carolyn.

Maya, Mandy, and Joy smiling at the camera. Click.

Mandy looked up adoringly at Serge. "I'll miss you, too, Serge. You have to come to Wyoming to visit me."

Does Mandy think Serge is her boyfriend, wondered Maya. Is he?

"I would like to visit the western part of America," Serge agreed. He glanced at his watch. "Now I have to go to work."

"We'll all walk you," offered Mandy. She looked around at the others. "Then I want to go to Madame Tussaud's Wax Museum. And tonight we're all going to Ivy's concert." She opened her arms to the sky. "I love every day in New York City."

Good for you, thought Joy. I'll love the day you're on a plane *leaving* New York City.

When they reached Zeus Tattoo and Piercing Parlor, Joy looked through the front window. She definitely wasn't going in if Wren was there. She wasn't.

"I'll go in first," Mandy announced, "so I can shoot Serge coming to work." She gestured toward the three girls. "You all come in after him. Look like you're interested in the store and like you've never been here before."

Joy peered through the storefront again. Still no Wren. But the minute they were all in the store, Wren came out from the back.

"The chick clique is here," she said cheerfully. She made a little wave and smiled right at Joy.

Joy didn't smile back.

Maya thought, Wren's not even a little bit embarrassed about what she did at Joy's. I wonder if she steals stuff all the time.

Meanwhile, Mandy introduced herself to Wren, explained that she was a friend of Serge's, and asked if she could film her.

"I'm leaving," Joy whispered to Maya and Carolyn. "I won't be in the same room as Wren. Not after what she did."

"Doesn't Mandy know about Wren's crashing the party and trying to steal Joy's ring?" Maya asked Carolyn.

"I never told her," explained Carolyn. "I didn't want to scare her about New York."

Joy rolled her eyes in Mandy's direction. She was shooting the piercings in Wren's tongue. "I think she could have handled it. So tell her. Okay?"

"Okay," promised Carolyn.

As Joy was leaving she heard Mandy say, "Wren, you have to come to my party." If Wren goes to that party, thought Joy, I'm not.

Mandy and Carolyn went alone to Madame Tussaud's Wax Museum. On the way, Carolyn told her about Wren and the party at Joy's apartment.

Carolyn loved the museum. There were nearly two hundred wax figures. She was surprised how many she recognized — Martin Luther King, Jr., the Dalai Lama, Albert Einstein. She liked the musicians best. Mandy kept asking her to take her picture with the wax figures.

Mandy with P. Diddy. Click.

Mandy with Eleanor Roosevelt. Click.

Mandy with Abraham Lincoln. Click.

Mandy videotaped Carolyn with the J-Lo interactive wax figure. It blushed.

"Let's do the Incredible Hulk, too," Mandy said as she led the way through the museum. "I read that he turns green. This will all be great for my film."

When they left the museum, they joined the tourist and rush hour traffic on the street and went into the 42nd Street subway station.

Carolyn checked her watch. They had just enough time to go home, grab something to eat, change their clothes, and take the subway back downtown for the concert. I'm sick of being busy every minute of the day, keeping up with Mandy's tourist schedule, she thought. I'm sick of the crowds, the noise, the summer heat, and the bad air.

They squeezed into an already crowded subway car. A woman shoved against Carolyn's shoulder to fit in behind her. A briefcase hit her leg. A wave of garlic breath blew in her face.

Whenever Carolyn felt overwhelmed by the city, she'd close her eyes for a second and imagine the open spaces and fresh air of the ranch. She'd think about her horse, her grandparents, and Mandy, and remind herself that they were all waiting for her whenever she wanted to move back. But that wasn't true anymore. Mandy had changed. She looked at her now — a pretty, bleached blond, hip, friendly teen, reading the subway announcement for a dermatologist named Dr. Zitz. My best friend has turned into a stranger, she thought. When I go to Wyoming — even for a visit — it won't be like it used to be. Mandy will be busy with Katrina and won't even want to ride.

Mandy's voice broke into her thoughts. "We'll take the Circle Line Tour tomorrow. It's a boat that goes all around Manhattan. I don't think I'll invite Joy. I mean, she's so negative. But maybe Maya will come."

"You can't invite one without inviting the other," Carolyn told her. "And I hope Wren doesn't come to the party. None of us like her."

"You're all way too sensitive about that ring business," said Mandy. "I bet Wren was just fooling around. Joy can't take a joke."

Joy has just about the best sense of humor of anybody I know, thought Carolyn. But she didn't bother to say that to Mandy. Mandy was going to believe whatever she wanted. That was the kind of girl she'd become.

Thursday morning, Joy waited outside the media center for Beth. There was something she needed to talk to her about — privately. When she spotted Beth coming down the block with a stack of books, she ran to meet her. Joy took two books off the pile, and they walked to the media center together.

"You're early," observed Beth.

"I have an idea I need to talk to you about," Joy explained.

They put the photography books on the workshop table. "Do you have an idea for the project you're embarrassed to talk about in front of the others?" Beth asked.

"That's not it." The knot of nervousness in Joy's belly tightened. "It's about how I'm helping in the workshop. You know, with Photoshop and the digital cameras. Everyone's going to need help with Photoshop for their projects. I could stay after class sometimes for that."

Beth opened one of the books to a place she'd marked with a Post-it. "That's a good idea. Do you mind doing it?"

"No. I just wondered if — since I'm helping out so much — if maybe I could have a scholarship just for this workshop because I'm helping. It's almost like I'm an assistant teacher. And remember, I'll be staying after to help with the projects, too," she said in all one breath.

Beth was staring at her.

Embarrassed, Joy glanced down at a photo in the open book.

A woman, arms outstretched in midair, like a bird. A baby — as big as the woman — hanging from her skirt, pulling her toward the earth.

"That picture was probably done in Photoshop," Joy said to break the silence and change the subject.

Beth touched her arm. "You're right, Joy. About the workshop fee. You shouldn't have to pay when you're helping. I should have thought of that myself."

Joy finally looked up. "So it's okay?"

Beth nodded. "But I still expect you to do the assignment."

"Sure," agreed Joy. As soon as Beth had turned away, a smile spread across Joy's face.

When Carolyn woke up Friday morning, Mandy was at the bureau putting on makeup. She had already showered and dressed in cutoffs and her Jay-Cee halter. "Okay, here's the schedule today," she announced as she brushed on mascara. "You get ready while I help Ivy with the dogs. I'll take care of inviting her to my party, too. When I get back, we'll take that Circle Line boat around Manhattan."

Carolyn sat up and rubbed the sleep out of her eyes. "Can't we take our time and go later?"

Mandy was at the door to their room. "No-o. I want to take the boat that leaves at ten. The whole thing takes three hours. After the boat tour, we're hitting the stores in Soho. There's this terrific makeup place I read about that gives free samples." Then she was gone.

After Maya took Naomi and Hannah to day camp and Piper to nursery school, she went to the park to take pictures of swings. She was glad that she'd said no to the boat tour. She was sick of running around doing tourist things with Mandy. Besides, it was expensive. Today she'd spend the whole day in her own neighborhood. Best of all, Shana was coming uptown after lunch and staying for a sleepover. They'd Rollerblade to the swimming pool in Central Park. Later, they'd pick up a couple of videos and the fixings for pizza. Shana loved to make pizza and was great at it. Her younger sisters were excited about that. She and Shana would bring their pizzas upstairs to her room. They'd eat, watch the videos, and talk. It would be a sleepover like they used to have. Before she started taking the photo workshop and met Joy and Carolyn. Before Shana got a boyfriend and moved to Brooklyn.

Maya turned on the digital camera, pushed an empty swing, shot a picture, and checked it on the screen. The swing wasn't high enough in the frame.

She tried again.

Empty swing midair. Click.

She replayed the shot. It was the one she wanted. Yes! Maya said to herself. Perfect.

On the way home, she stopped at the Italian deli to buy mozzarella cheese, pepperoni, and dough for the pizzas. The next stop was the produce market for mushrooms — Shana liked those. They'd use some basil from Grandma Josie's herb garden.

She was putting pizza fixings in the refrigerator

when she noticed a note stuck to the door with a smiley-face magnet. It read MAYA, CALL SHANA.

She called Shana.

Shana canceled out of dinner and the sleepover.

Joy sat on the couch in her bedroom and turned her camera over in her hands. What can I do for my project? she wondered. Should I use a memory? A dream? How about a nightmare? I've had plenty of those.

The images of one of her childhood nightmares popped into her mind. She'd had it again and again as a little kid.

She always wakes up because she thinks there's something evil in her room. Terrified, she looks around in the dark. Maybe a monster came in through a window. But the windows in her room are closed. What about the closet? She didn't check in there before she went to bed. By the glow of her ballerina night-light, she sees that the closet door is open a crack. Did a monster slither out of the closet? Will it crawl into her bed? If she shouts for her parents, the monster will gobble her up, for sure. If she runs out of the room, it'll chase her. She has to hide. How about under the bed? Still in the nightmare, she quietly slips to the floor and gets on her hands and knees. She lifts the bed skirt to crawl under. A huge, green snakelike monster with red eyes is staring right at her.

Joy shivered with the memory. I always woke up from that nightmare screaming, she remembered.

It always seemed superreal because I was in bed in the nightmare, too.

I need to put that scared feeling in a picture, she thought. First, I need photos of under the bed. She sat on the floor near her bed and turned on the camera. There is no monster under there, she had to remind herself as she lifted the bed skirt to take pictures.

She was online looking for pictures of monsters to use for her dream photo when her cell phone rang.

It was Maya.

A computer-generated, purple snakelike monster popped up on the monitor. "Hi," she said to Maya. "How's it going?"

"Okay," answered Maya. "What are you doing?"

Joy described her idea for the workshop project and the purple snake on her monitor. "But this monster isn't right," she commented as she replaced it with a dragon spitting fire. That wasn't the monster of her nightmare, either. "How's your project coming?" she asked Maya.

Maya described the photos she'd taken of the swing. "My grandmother said there's a black-and-white photo of me running toward the camera when I was around three years old. She's going to look for it."

A green, red-eyed serpentine monster faced Joy on the computer. A shiver ran through her. She saved the image to a file.

"I'm glad you called," she told Maya. She hesitated a second before asking, "Do you want to come over?"

"I have to make dinner for my sisters tonight," Maya answered.

"That's all right," Joy said, embarrassed that she had asked. She'd never invited Maya without Carolyn. It's always the three of them or — when Maya was busy — just her and Carolyn.

"But I can still come over," Maya added. "I just meant I have to get home by, like, six o'clock."

"Okay," said Joy. A very fierce-looking two-headed gray creature with blood dripping out its mouths filled the screen. She closed the monster picture file. "I'm going to wait until you get here to look at any more of these. I'm scaring myself."

"I'm on my way." Maya hung up the phone and thought, I'm glad I have something to do besides sit around being mad at Shana. How could Shana cancel at the last minute like that? Just because Alex invited her to go to Coney Island. I hate when girls do that. She put her Rollerblades back in the closet. I suppose she'll bring Alex to Mandy's party on Sunday, too. Can't she do anything without her boyfriend?

Carolyn faced a wall of mirrors. Her hair looked limp. No wonder, she thought. It's, like, a hundred degrees outside. She looked away from her own reflection and met herself in another mirror over a counter of lipsticks. Everywhere she looked in this store there were mirrors. And makeup. Counter after counter of makeup.

"I'm going to have a makeup session at the Purr-fect Faces counter," Mandy told her. "They'll do it for free, even if you don't buy anything. It said so in the guidebook."

As Carolyn trailed behind Mandy, her cell phone rang. She pulled it out of her bag and opened it. It must be her father checking up on her.

A woman's voice said, "Hello."

M. G.? wondered Carolyn.

"Is Mandy there?" the voice asked.

It wasn't M. G. She wouldn't be calling Mandy.

Mandy was perched on a high stool at the Purr-fect Faces counter. A fake redhead with a name tag that read BELLE was cleansing Mandy's face.

"Mandy's sort of busy right now," Carolyn told whoever was calling her.

"It must be Katrina," Mandy said as she put out her hand for the phone. Carolyn handed it to her.

Carolyn picked up a sample lipstick and applied a short stripe of color to the back of her left hand. Too red.

"Do you *have* to go, Kat?" Mandy was saying.

Carolyn opened another lipstick and put a slippery mark next to the first.

Too brown.

How come Katrina has my dad's cell phone number? Carolyn wondered as she opened another lipstick.

"That lipstick would look good with your hair,"

Belle remarked, "and would be a bold statement. Try it."

Mandy snapped the phone closed.

Carolyn used a tiny shovel-shaped applicator to scrape off some of the lipstick. She looked into the mirror to apply it to her lips. Mandy was reflected behind her.

"Katrina's going to Norway for the rest of the summer," Mandy's reflection told Carolyn's reflection. "To visit her grandmother. It's going to completely ruin our plans. We were supposed to edit my New York City video together."

"Too bad," Carolyn said without meaning it. Who cared if Mandy's plans were ruined? The color of the lipstick clashed with her hair.

"How's that lipstick?" Belle asked.

"I don't like it," answered Carolyn as she wiped it off.

At Home

Early Sunday morning, Carolyn woke to the sound of rain spattering against the window. She closed her eyes and snuggled deeper into her pillow. Good, she thought, it's raining. Maybe Mandy won't be in such a hurry to go out. She opened her eyes again with a start. It was Sunday! The day of Mandy's party. If the rain kept up, they couldn't have a picnic.

An hour later Mandy, Carolyn, and her father listened to the weather forecast while they ate breakfast. The unexpected storm was sticking around for the day. The party would have to be inside.

"It'll be a fun party, anyway," Mandy told Dr. Kuhlberg. "Everyone who is coming is so great." She winked at Carolyn. "I especially like Ivy."

Carolyn's dad looked up from reading the newspaper. "A talented young woman," he agreed.

Carolyn didn't bother to remind him again that Ivy was almost as old as he was. It was probably a bad idea to set them up, anyway.

After breakfast, Carolyn went out to finish her errands while Mandy called everyone to tell them to come to the apartment instead of the park.

First, Carolyn went to the bakery for a dozen fresh bagels. Next, to the deli for ice.

When she walked back into the apartment, her father and Mandy were standing at the counter grinning at her.

"What's up?" she asked.

"Do you want the good news or the bad news?" Mandy asked.

"The bad news."

Mandy's grin slipped into a frown. "The bad news is that Ivy can't come to the party. She's got a really bad cold. And Wren's not coming. She has to work."

If Wren's not coming, that's the *good* news, thought Carolyn. She opened the freezer door to put in the ice.

"Don't you want to know the good news?" asked Mandy.

"I thought you just told me," Carolyn answered.

"The *good* news is I'm staying here for at least *four more weeks*!" Mandy announced. "While you were out, your dad talked to my parents. Everybody said it was okay."

Carolyn was so surprised by the so-called good news that the bag of ice slipped out of her hands. She caught it before it hit the floor, stuffed it into the crowded freezer, and closed the door.

"There is so much to see and do in New York City," continued Mandy.

Carolyn turned to Mandy and forced a smile. "Wow. That is a surprise."

"And I can work more on my tape. Katrina said I'd be stupid to go home now. I mean, she's not even going to be there."

"I'm glad you're staying, Mandy," Carolyn's father said. "You girls have always been like sisters."

Not anymore, thought Carolyn.

"So it's not a going-away party after all, which will make it even more fun," said Mandy. She glanced at the clock. "I better take my shower."

When Mandy was gone Carolyn thought, I have to tell Dad I don't want Mandy to stay. "Dad, I —" she began.

"You don't have to thank me," he said, interrupting her. "I don't mind having Mandy around. I want you to have a good summer." He looked at his watch. "I'm meeting Maxine to go over some research. I'll be back for the party. It's only kids now, right?"

Carolyn mentally ran through the list of who was coming to the party. If Ivy wasn't going to be there, her dad was the only adult. "Right," she agreed.

"Then I'll just be there to supervise," he said. "I have some work I need to do, anyway."

"Will you stay in your room though? I mean, if you don't mind."

"I will," he agreed. "But I'll be checking in on you guys every once in a while." He gave his daughter a quick kiss on the forehead.

As soon as Carolyn was alone, hot angry tears sprang to her eyes. *How could Mandy decide to stay without asking me first? Don't I have to say that it's okay? After all, it's my room she's sharing. My drawers and closet she's hogging. My time she takes up every minute of every day with her plans. My friends. Can't Dad tell I'm sick of having Mandy around?* The tears overflowed. *Mom would have known.*

Mandy shouted from the bedroom, "Hey, Carolyn, can I borrow that cute sundress with the pink trim?"

That's the dress *I* was going to wear, thought Carolyn.

"Okay, I guess," she called back to Mandy.

Mandy filmed the guests as they arrived.

Serge came first. While Carolyn put the pierogies on a plate, Mandy told him her big news. He thought it was great. "There is time now to show to you Coney Island on the day I don't work."

Shana and Alex arrived next. They brought soda. Shana introduced Alex to Mandy and he did a break-dance move for the camera. When Shana heard that Mandy was staying, she was happy, too. "You'll be here for the next poetry slam."

"I'll tape it!" exclaimed Mandy.

Ousmane came in with some bite-sized barbecued chicken pieces and a peanut sauce to dip them in. Maya was next with brownies she'd made that morning. Jay-Cee came with freshly popped popcorn. Carolyn was pouring the popcorn into a big bowl when Mandy told Ousmane, Maya, and Jay-Cee that she was staying longer.

While Jay-Cee and Mandy hugged over the news,

Maya checked Carolyn's reaction. She isn't happy about it, Maya decided. So why did she ask her to stay?

Joy came next. She brought cream cheese for the bagels and ice cream for the brownies. When she saw the camera, she put up a hand to block it. "Mandy, I told you not to shoot me without asking."

"Oops," said Mandy as she turned off the camera and backed away. "I forgot. Sorry. I just wanted to get everyone coming to my party."

"Well, I'm not staying if Wren's here," announced Joy. She looked around to see if Wren was lurking someplace. Or was she already in Carolyn's room pocketing jewelry?

"Wren's not coming," Carolyn said. Mandy, she saw, was in the kitchen area taking the ice out of the freezer and putting in the ice cream.

"Mandy's staying for another four weeks," Maya whispered to Joy.

Joy poked Carolyn in the arm. "Why did you invite her?"

"I didn't," protested Carolyn. "She invited herself and got my dad to say it was okay before she even told me. I can't tell her she can't stay."

"Why not?" asked Joy.

Maya looked from Joy to Carolyn.

"It'd be so rude. And my dad thinks it's like this big favor to me that he's letting her stay."

"So tell *him*," insisted Joy.

"That's not so easy," Carolyn protested. "Then what's he supposed to do?"

"We have to talk about this, Carolyn," said Maya.

"Hey, you guys," Mandy called from the kitchen. "No secrets. Come on. We're all going to dance." She smiled up at Serge. "I bet you're a great dancer."

"Let's meet in Carolyn's room," whispered Maya. "Joy, you go first. I'll come next. Then Carolyn."

Shana put on some hip-hop CD she'd brought. Alex and Shana danced together. Mandy taught Serge, Jay-Cee, and Ousmane a move that was all bent knees and hips. Where'd she learn to dance like that? wondered Carolyn. Did Katrina teach her?

No one was looking at Joy, so she slipped off to Carolyn's room.

Maya and Carolyn went into the kitchen. Maya arranged brownies on a plate, then left.

Mandy was teaching Alex and Shana the dance move, too. Carolyn watched for a minute before sneaking off. Maya and Joy were waiting for her.

"She can't just stay if you don't want her here," said Joy.

"She's my best friend," protested Carolyn. "I mean she was my best friend."

"Aren't you sick of following her around and helping her with that stupid movie?" asked Joy.

Carolyn nodded. She looked nervously toward the doorway to make sure no one was there. "I haven't had a minute to do anything but be a tour guide since she got here." She gestured toward three books on her desk. "I haven't even started on the summer reading list we got from school. And my project for the workshop? Forget about it."

"You can't let her push you around anymore," said Joy. "She's too bossy."

"Joy's right," agreed Maya. "Tell Mandy you have your own stuff to do. Don't just do what she wants. If she doesn't have anyone to hang out with, maybe she'll get bored and go home."

Joy shook her head. "That'll take too long. CK, you should just tell her to go home now."

"Could you do that if you were me?" asked Carolyn.

"If I were you, I'd be too sweet to tell her to go. Me as me? I could do it."

Carolyn arched her eyebrow Joy-style. "Right. You're real tough."

Maya put an arm around Carolyn and gave her a little hug. "So stop going everywhere with Mandy. If she calls us, we won't have time to do anything with her, either."

"That's easy," agreed Joy.

Carolyn's father appeared at the doorway. "Is something wrong?" he asked.

"No, Dad," Carolyn said. "We were just talking."

"It was hard to talk out there with the music," explained Maya.

"We're going back now," added Joy.

Maya led the way out of Carolyn's room. Mandy had stopped dancing and was looking around. She's wondering where we all went, thought Maya. Does she know we're talking about her?

As Joy left Carolyn's room she glanced around. It was cluttered with piles of clothes, makeup, and video equipment. All Mandy's. This room is smaller than Jake's new room, she thought. How can Carolyn stand sharing it? Especially with Mandy.

The next morning, Mandy slept in while Carolyn walked the dogs with Ivy. Ivy wanted to know all about the party.

"It was okay," Carolyn said. She hesitated before adding, "Mandy's staying for another four weeks."

Ivy turned to her. "How do you feel about that? It doesn't seem to me that you've been too happy about her visit."

A lump came up Carolyn's throat. Ivy understood she'd been unhappy. Carolyn told her how Mandy had changed and how it upset her. "And now she wants to stay," Carolyn concluded.

"It's a tricky situation," agreed Ivy. "I'm sorry."

Precious licked Carolyn's hand. She patted his head. "It's okay. It's only a few more weeks."

"You know the saying," added Ivy. "'After three days, socks and company stink.'"

Carolyn laughed. "But socks are easier to get rid of."

When Carolyn came back to the apartment, Mandy was dressed and ready to go out. "I need to shoot on the Upper East Side and then go to Chinatown. We still haven't been there yet."

"I need to stay home today," Carolyn told her. "I want to work on my project." She pointed to the books on her desk. "And I have to start my summer reading for school."

Mandy looked disappointed. "I guess I'll ask Maya," she said. "Maybe she can go with me."

"Maybe," Carolyn agreed.

Mandy picked up the phone. A minute later she reported, "Maya's busy, too."

Mandy tried Shana next. She wasn't home.

Carolyn was looking through the summer reading books. "Shana works at a day camp for kids," she said without looking up. "And Jay-Cee works at Remember Me."

"Serge has his English class," observed Mandy. She slung her orange messenger bag over her shoulder. "I'll just go to the East Side by myself."

"Clear it with my dad, first," Carolyn reminded her.

A few minutes later, Mandy left with her camera and Carolyn's father's cell phone.

An hour after she left, Carolyn was on chapter two of the novel, and it started to rain — hard.

Joy was reading in her room, too. Hip-hop was playing on the radio.

"Joy," she heard her mother shout above the music. She looked up to see her mother standing in the doorway in her bathrobe. Joy reached over and turned down the volume on the radio. "They rang from the lobby," her mother announced. "Someone is on the way up."

"Who?" asked Joy.

"Mandy. That friend of Carolyn's."

Mandy? Carolyn must be with her, Joy thought as she went to the front of the apartment. I guess she couldn't keep her promise not to hang out with her. Carolyn is too nice sometimes. But when she opened the door, only Mandy came in. Joy didn't know what to ask first — "Where's Carolyn?" or "Why are you here?"

Mandy answered both questions before Joy could decide. "Carolyn has to work on her project so I'm on my own today. I was in your neighborhood when it started to rain. I remembered that you have a good computer." She held up a disk. "I have my Final Cut Pro editing software and the cable I need. I'll delete my stuff off your hard drive when I'm done. Can I use your computer to edit? "

"I guess," answered Joy.

As soon as Mandy was set up at the computer, Joy went to the kitchen to call Carolyn with the news.

"You should have just told her she couldn't use your computer," Carolyn said.

"Could you have done that?" asked Joy.

"If I were you I could have," teased Carolyn. "Me as me? I couldn't do it."

"It's not easy to say no to Mandy," said Joy.

*   *   *

At the photo workshop on Tuesday, Mandy demonstrated her Final Cut Pro editing program to the class. When the workshop session was over, Carolyn and Maya told Mandy they had to go right home to work on their projects, and Joy said she'd be working on her computer. "That's okay," Mandy said. "I'm going over to Zeus to hang out with Serge and Wren. Serge wants to introduce me to the owner."

"Ivan," said Carolyn and Maya in unison.

Mandy smiled. "Right. Well, Serge said Ivan will let me interview him for the video. Cool, huh?"

Mandy went east on Eighth Street while Carolyn, Maya, and Joy went west toward the subway.

"The plan isn't working," Carolyn admitted to Joy. "Mandy's still having a good time."

"Don't give up," said Maya. "We can't give up."

"I still think you have to tell her to go home," added Joy.

Carolyn gave her the arched-eyebrow look. "Like you did yesterday?"

"Good point, CK," laughed Maya.

"You guys," Carolyn said. "This is serious. I can't take three and a half more weeks of Mandy. You have to help me."

"Get her to come to the workshop on Thursday," suggested Maya. "And we'll all work on her." She turned to Joy. "Can you hang out after?"

Joy nodded. "But how are we going to get her to leave?"

They walked along thinking to themselves.

Maya broke the silence. "Okay. Here's an idea. We get her to talk about Wyoming. Ask her lots of questions so she gets homesick."

"That's good," said Carolyn. "She loves it back there. Well, she used to."

"What if that doesn't work?" asked Joy.

"If that doesn't work we'll — uh —" Maya stammered. "Oh, I don't know. I can't think of anything."

"Me, either," Carolyn put in. She sighed. "It's hopeless."

"But we have to try," added Maya.

The next day, Maya worked at Remember Me until it was time to pick up her sisters at day camp. Shana was coming for dinner and a sleepover. If Shana actually shows up this time, thought Maya, I'm going to tell her that I hate it when girls cancel dates with their girlfriends to be with their boyfriends.

As Maya was going up the front steps with her sisters, she heard a familiar voice coming through the open windows of her grandmother's apartment. Mandy? She went back down the stairs and looked through the shutters into the front room. Mandy was shooting Josie. Maya backed away before Mandy saw her. What if Mandy stays? she thought. If she's here when Shana comes, will Shana invite her to stay? Will she invite her to sleep over?

Maya phoned Carolyn to see if she knew that Mandy was uptown. She didn't. The instant Maya put the phone down, it rang. It was Shana saying she was on her way. Five minutes later, Mandy came into the kitchen from the inside stairs that connected Josie's apartment to the second floor. "Surprise!"

Naomi jumped up from her snack to hug her.

Piper yelled, "I want to be in the movie."

Maya leaned against the kitchen counter and folded her arms. Don't be too nice, she cautioned herself, or she'll never leave. But there was nothing she could do about her younger sisters' excitement.

Hannah held up her Hannah's Beauty Salon box. "Can I braid your hair again? It's Wednesday. That's an extra-discount day."

"Shana's making pizza for us," added Naomi. "She makes the best."

"I'd love to stay," said Mandy.

Maya's heart fell. I've got to tell her no, she thought. But how?

"Except I can't," Mandy continued. "I left Carolyn alone all day." She smiled at Maya. "She's getting to be a stick-in-the-mud."

Maya smiled back. "That sounds like something her grandfather would say."

"Exactly," agreed Mandy. "Her grandfather is so great. I miss him. Sorry about not being able to stay."

"That's okay," said Maya. She put an arm around Naomi's shoulder. "We'll manage."

Carolyn looked at the photos spread across her desk. She'd raided her photo album for them.

Mandy and Carolyn at four with their first ponies.
Mandy's first-grade school picture.
Mandy dressed as a clown for Halloween.

Carolyn studied the photos through a magnifier. In each one there was a sweet expression on Mandy's face. Carolyn turned on the digital camera and went through the photos she'd taken of Mandy during the visit. She concentrated on the close-ups. Was the sweet expression still there?

"I'm back," Mandy called from the front room. Carolyn quickly turned off the camera and pushed the photos under her pile of books.

Mandy came in and threw herself across the bed. "What a great day," she gushed. "I love Josie."

Carolyn turned toward her. "What'd she talk about?"

"Astrology. It was so interesting."

"Did you tell her you were a Pisces?" asked Carolyn.

Mandy nodded. "She said it's a time in my life for adventure. So I guess I'm doing the right thing being in New York this summer."

Thanks a lot, Josie, thought Carolyn.

Chinatown

Maya had all the ingredients for the pizzas out when Shana arrived.

Naomi and Piper danced around Shana shouting, "Pizza! Pizza!" But Hannah stood back, looking unhappy.

Shana went over to her. "What's wrong, Hannah?"

Hannah held her hair salon shoe box to her chest and grumbled, "Your hair."

Shana rubbed her hand along her freshly braided cornrows. "You don't like it? I just had it done."

Hannah kicked the tile floor with her sneaker toe. "I wanted to do it."

Shana put an arm around her. "Next time I come, you can. Okay?"

Hannah took the appointment book out of her box. Shana picked out a date two months away when she'd let Hannah do her hair. Will it be that long before I see her again? Maya wondered.

Maya's parents and sisters ate the homemade pizzas in the kitchen, but Shana and Maya took theirs to Maya's bedroom. Maya hung a hotel DO NOT DIS-

TURB sign on her doorknob and closed the door behind them. Finally, she and Shana were alone. Now maybe they could talk — just the two of them.

They put on their favorite radio station and sat cross-legged facing each other. They talked about Shana's job, the slam poetry team, her room in her aunt's apartment, her new school, and Alex. Finally, Maya asked, "How's your mom doing?"

"Okay, I guess."

Maya noticed that Shana had stopped eating. She put down her own half-eaten slice. "Do you ever see her?"

"I went to visit her. It was this forever bus ride." She gazed out the window. "It was awful there. I mean everyone is so — I don't know — out of it."

"Including your mom?" prodded Maya.

Shana looked out the window. "Yeah. Including my mom. But she was calmer. She didn't yell at me or anything. She kept introducing me to her new friends." Her gaze returned to Maya. "I guess that's good. I mean that she's got friends."

"Having friends is always good," agreed Maya.

Maya imagined how she'd feel if her mother hit her and yelled at her. And if her mother had a mental illness and had to go to a special hospital? That would be so hard. She felt tears coming to her eyes. "I'm really sorry all this has happened to you, Shana," she said. "It's just so awful."

Shana put up her hands. "Hey, wow! Hold on there. I don't need sympathy. Or pity. That's way weird. The great thing about Alex is he doesn't make a big deal about it." She picked up her slice again. "End of discussion."

Maya looked down so that Shana wouldn't see her blinking away the tears. Why can't I get along with Shana anymore? she wondered. Why do I keep saying the wrong thing?

Mandy went to the workshop with Carolyn on Thursday. But instead of sitting with Carolyn, Mandy sat between Janice and Ousmane. The three of them seemed to be having a great old time. What if Mandy never goes home? Carolyn wondered. What if she stays all summer? She remembered how she and Mandy used to beg to have Mandy move to the ranch. They wrote a petition to their parents listing the reasons they wanted to live as sisters. The first was "We'll always have a friend to be with so we won't be lonely." Another was "We're not real sisters so we'll never fight."

The adults had not agreed with the plan. But Mandy slept over a lot more after that. We had so much fun, thought Carolyn. That's when we started pretending we were sisters and calling each other M-Sis and C-Sis. We'd say things like "Hey, C-Sis, what should we do next?"

"Earth to Carolyn," Beth said, startling her from her daydream.

Carolyn made a little wave in Beth's direction. "Sorry."

"You seem to do well in the daydreaming department," Beth said. Are you putting some of that into your photography? What's your subject?"

"I don't have one yet," admitted Carolyn. "I've been really busy this summer."

Mandy held up her hand. "It's my fault. I've been taking up a lot of her time."

Carolyn and Maya exchanged a surprised look.

"But now that I know more people in New York," continued Mandy, "Carolyn will have time to do her own thing." She turned to Carolyn. "And I can help you with your project. If you want. We have a lot of the same memories."

Do we? wondered Carolyn. You don't act like you remember anything about being friends.

After class, the four girls took the subway to Chinatown. When they came out into the street, Mandy linked one arm through Joy's arm and the other through Maya's. "I've been missing you guys."

"I guess we've all been pretty busy," said Joy. She exchanged a look with Maya behind Mandy's head. It was time to start Operation Homesick.

"What's it like in Wyoming in the summer?" asked Maya. "Is it hot like this?"

"Not this bad," observed Mandy. "And, of course, the air is cleaner."

They stopped for the light. Bumper-to-bumper cabs, trucks, and cars moved slowly along Canal Street. A horn honked. A police car, its light turning and siren blaring, weaved through the traffic.

"It must be a lot quieter in Wyoming," observed Joy. "And peaceful."

They started across Canal Street. "It is," agreed Mandy. "Hey, did you know that Canal Street used to be a real canal? A lot of the west side of Lower Manhattan used to be underwater. No one lived down there but fish. And that includes where Battery Park City is now."

Maya imagined Lower Manhattan underwater.

"I didn't know that," admitted Carolyn.

Colorful storefront signs and awnings covered in Chinese characters lined both sides of Canal Street. The sidewalks were so crowded with people and crates piled high with merchandise that the girls had to walk single file.

Mandy took out her camera.

It was hard to talk about Wyoming when they were walking behind one another and Mandy was shooting.

Joy led them to a big Chinese department store. Maya whispered into Carolyn's ear, "Remember, Operation Homesick."

Carolyn noticed a large Chinese painting of craggy, snow-covered mountains hanging above them. She pointed it out to Mandy. "Don't those mountains remind you of the Tetons back home?"

"Sort of," agreed Mandy.

"You must miss the mountains and the wide-open spaces," commented Joy.

Mandy moved aside to let three women speaking in Chinese pass down the narrow aisle. "I love all the different kinds of people in New York," she said. "It's like the whole world is here."

Joy looked at Carolyn and shook her head to say, "That didn't work." She glanced around the store. What else could they try to make Mandy homesick? She remembered that Mandy had an older brother with twin baby girls. She must miss them. "Let's check out the toys," she said with a wink to Carolyn. "I want to find a present for Jake."

"Okay," Carolyn agreed, not sure what Joy had in mind.

As they walked through the toy section, Joy picked out a box of animal finger puppets. "This is perfect for Jake. I can make up stories for him." She handed the box to Mandy. "Do you want to buy one of these for your nieces?"

"You must miss them," added Carolyn, finally catching on to Joy's idea. "Those girls are so cute."

"They're adorable," agreed Mandy. "But I hardly ever see them. They moved to Oregon, remember?" She handed the puppets back to Joy. "I better not buy these. Now that I'm staying longer I have to make my money last. My parents are sending me more, but — wow — New York is expensive."

"It's a problem," agreed Joy. "I bet you don't spend so much back home."

"If you were home you could probably save up to buy your own video camera," added Maya.

"True," agreed Mandy. "But here I'm having new and interesting experiences. That's worth a lot."

Joy and Maya exchanged a glance that said, "Operation Homesick fails."

Joy bought the finger puppets for Jake. Maya got jasmine incense for her grandmother. Mandy found eye shadow the same shade that the makeup artist at Purr-fect Faces had used, but at half the price. Carolyn bought a pink lipstick.

"My guidebook said to get buns from this Chinese bakery," Mandy announced as they were leaving the store. "They don't cost much. Let's get some."

"Okay," agreed Carolyn. She'd never had Chinese buns, and she was hungry. Sometimes Mandy had good ideas.

They bought a bag of sweet buns and ate them as they walked through the rest of Chinatown.

At four o'clock, Maya said she had to head home. She turned to Joy. "Are you going to your mom's or are you staying downtown?"

"My mom's," answered Joy. "I'll go up with you guys and take the crosstown bus."

Carolyn pointed to the green globe light of a subway station on the corner. "There's the stop where we got off," she announced. "We're back where we started."

"Wait a sec," Mandy said. "I need a bottle of water." She looked around at them. "Anyone else?"

"I'll go with you," offered Maya.

Joy and Carolyn waited on the corner while Mandy and Maya went into a small shop.

Joy wiped sweat from her forehead with a clean napkin from the bun bag. "It's so hot! I mean it's *hot*. Mandy's crazy to want to stay here."

The acrid smell of rotten food drifted around Carolyn. She looked down at a pile of black garbage bags near the curb. I should have gone to Wyoming for the summer, she thought. Dad said I could. My grandparents wanted me to. I would have spent the summer riding, helping out with the ranch, and hanging out with my Wyoming friends. Not Mandy. My other friends. Or have they all changed, too?

The four girls held on to the center pole of the crowded subway car. Maya didn't care that they didn't have seats. She was just happy to be in air-conditioning. Soon she'd be home in her own air-conditioned room. Maybe tonight she'd call Shana. In the end they'd had a good enough time watching a favorite old movie and talking about all their friends from the neighborhood. I just can't say too much about her mom, she decided.

Joy was lost in her thoughts, too. Thoughts about her dad's new apartment. Her dad and Sue still hadn't completely unpacked. "Where are we supposed to put all this stuff?" Sue had complained as she pushed boxes of books, an extra set of dishes, and winter clothes into Jake's room. Those boxes took up all the floor space where I would have put the air mattress, thought Joy.

Carolyn was worrying about what to do for her project.

Suddenly, the train screeched to a stop and the lights dimmed. It was almost dark. Carolyn looked out the window. They were still in the subway tunnel, not a station. An old woman sitting near her sighed.

A few people grumbled complaints.

A little boy asked loudly, "How come it stopped, Mommy?"

"Because it's the New York subway system," a stranger sitting across from the boy's mother answered for her. "They raised the fares, and the service is still no good."

A few people laughed, including Joy.

The boy's mother told her son the train would move pretty soon and that he should be a good boy. Carolyn saw that she had another child with her — an infant in a stroller.

"The air-conditioning is off," a woman next to the young mother commented to a friend on the other side of her. "Listen. Do you hear it?"

"No," agreed the friend. "I don't feel it, either."

"There's no electricity on the train," the elderly woman said with alarm. "We've lost power."

"Some of the lights are working," observed another.

"Those are emergency lights," a big guy standing near the door explained. "They don't use juice from the grid."

"Man, am I going to be late for my baseball game?" a teenage boy asked no one in particular.

In a frightened voice, the little boy said, "It's dark, Mommy. How come it's *dark*?"

"I don't know, Todd," she answered. Carolyn could hear the alarm in the mother's voice.

Mandy squatted in front of the boy. "There's a little problem with the subway," she said in a super-calm voice. "Someone is going to fix it. Do you like to fix things?"

"I fix my truck," the boy answered. "The wheel comes off."

Carolyn smelled smoke. Was there a fire in the tunnel?

"Hey, put that out," someone shouted.

Carolyn saw that the smoke was from a man smoking a cigarette at the other end of a car.

"Hey, if he's smoking, I'm lighting up, too," a woman called out.

A few people told the guy with the cigarette to put it out.

"Just do it," Joy added to the chorus.

"Mind your own business," the smoker shouted back.

"NO SMOKING!" a deep male voice shouted. "You start a fire in here and we're in a furnace. No electricity means the doors won't work."

"Besides, where d'ya think we're getting fresh air

in here, anyway, with it all closed up?" added another voice. "We're using up all the oxygen just *breathing*."

The guy threw the cigarette on the floor and ground it out with the toe of his shoe.

"It already feels like a furnace," someone called out.

A few people laughed. But not many.

Are we going to suffocate? Carolyn wondered. Sweat seeped through her T-shirt, which stuck to her back. She pulled off her backpack and put it on the floor between her feet.

"Why don't they make an announcement or something?" a woman asked, her voice shaky with fear.

"No electricity," three voices answered in unison.

Again, a few laughs. Nervous laughs.

"I'm sure we'll be moving soon," Mandy said in a voice loud enough for everyone around her to hear.

"Who made you the expert?"

Carolyn looked around to see who said it. *The guy who lit the cigarette. I don't like him.*

Joy wiped sweat off her forehead with the already damp bun napkin.

The infant cried its discomfort. The woman took the baby out of the stroller. "Get her juice out of the bag," she directed the boy.

"I want juice, too," he whined.

Mandy reached into the bag hanging off the stroller and handed the woman a baby bottle. The little boy fidgeted and repeated his demand for juice and complained that he was hungry, too.

Mandy pulled her camera out of her orange bag.

"What's that?" Todd asked.

"My video camera," she answered. She smiled at his mother. "Can I film him?"

"Anything to hush him up," the mother agreed.

While Mandy taped the little boy, Carolyn checked out the rest of the people on the subway. A few tried to read by the emergency lighting but were mostly giving up. One woman kept trying to call on her cell phone. Over and over.

"You're just wasting your battery power," the man next to her observed. "You may need it when we get out of here."

"*If* we get out of here," someone added.

A man got up to give a not-too-pregnant pregnant woman a seat. After that, a few others offered seats to people who looked like they needed them more than they did.

"Smoking Guy isn't budging off his comfy seat," Joy whispered to Carolyn.

Someone started praying out loud. A few people told him to shut up.

"It's the end of the world," the Prayer Man shouted. "You better pray for forgiveness for your sins, brother. Judgment Day is upon us."

"Keep it to yourself, buddy," someone said in a kinder voice.

The man continued to pray but lowered his voice to a harsh whisper.

What if something really horrible has happened

above ground, Carolyn wondered, *like a nuclear bomb. Who would tell us? We could all be here until we died.*

A woman sang the song "New York, New York" in an angry voice, changing some of the words to express her complaints about the subway system.

> *Start spreading the news, I'm leaving today.*
> *I want to be no part of it — New York, New York.*
> *These vagabond shoes are longing to stray*
> *Right out of the very heart of it — this dead subway.*

The way the woman sang the song frightened Carolyn. Especially when she sang it over and over. *Is that woman a little crazy?* she wondered. *A lot crazy?*

Time crept slowly on. Ten minutes, fifteen minutes, a half hour. As they waited in the hot semi-darkness for someone to rescue them, Joy was more and more certain that there'd been another terrorist attack on the city. What was going on above ground? Would they ever get out alive?

Maya could feel the worry and panic growing all around her — particularly in Joy. She reached out and touched Joy's arm. Joy turned to her. Even in the dim light, Maya could see the fear in her eyes. "We'll stick together," Maya whispered to her. "All of four of us. No matter what happens."

Joy nodded her agreement.

Before Maya could include Carolyn and Mandy

in the vow, the door between cars opened and a conductor entered the car. Dozens of questions were thrown at her.

The woman put up her hand. "Hold on, folks. Just listen, okay? We have a blackout situation here."

More questions tumbled over one another.

"I'm going to tell you if you'll listen."

Except for Smoking Guy shouting an obscenity, everyone was quiet.

"We've got a blackout. All of New York City. Maybe upstate, too. No power, the trains don't run. That's why we're all sitting here."

"Terrorists!" the young mother gasped.

A scattering of moans and cries came from all directions.

"Not again," the old woman moaned.

The train worker held up her hand again and waited for everyone to quiet down. "No," she said. "They don't think it's terrorists. But we're not sure what caused it. The important thing is to stay calm. We'll get you out. Now let me through so I can tell the cars behind you."

As the conductor squeezed past Carolyn, she noticed the sweat dripping down her face.

What isn't she telling us? What else does she know?

Broadway / Seventh Avenue Local

Carolyn glanced down at the elderly woman. She returned Carolyn's gaze with a frightened look. "My husband," she said in a shaky voice. "He's alone. He's been sick. I was going to see my sister. I shouldn't have left him alone. I shouldn't have."

"I'm sure he'll be all right," Carolyn said. "We'll be out of here pretty soon."

"How do you know that?" Anger crept into the woman's voice.

Carolyn studied her pink sneakers. Tears filled her eyes. She blinked them back and turned to see Mandy looking at her. No matter how brave Mandy is acting, thought Carolyn, she must be scared, too. She leaned toward Mandy and whispered, "We'll get out."

Mandy nodded and whispered back, "Thanks, C-Sis."

C-Sis. That's the first time Mandy's called me that since she got here. A flashback: Mandy and I are horseback riding in the hills behind the ranch with Charlie Olson. A snake spooks my horse and he rears. I'm thrown from the saddle and break my leg. Charlie rides back for help. Mandy stays with me and keeps

123

me warm and safe for two hours. I was scared then, too. But it was better because Mandy was there.

Carolyn turned back to the elderly woman and leaned over her. "I'm sorry about your husband."

The woman patted Carolyn's hand. "Thank you. I'm sorry I snapped at you. You were just being kind."

"That's okay," Carolyn said.

"My name is Rose," the woman said.

Maya moved over to the pregnant woman and offered her water.

Joy squatted in front of a young girl who was crying and told her everything would be okay. "The woman who came through said so, and she works for the subways."

The girl twisted the strap of her backpack. "My mother gets so mad when I'm late."

"Your mother knows there's a blackout," Joy said. "So she knows it's not your fault you're late." She dug into her bag and offered the girl the last bun. The girl leaned across the man next to her and handed it to the little boy.

Mandy and Joy exchanged a smile.

The conductor opened the door again. "Okay, folks. We're going to walk through four cars to the front. Let's be orderly. Children and seniors first."

"Can't you get this thing running?" complained Smoking Guy. "How am I supposed to get home?"

A few people told him to be quiet. Someone said, "We're all in the same boat, buddy."

"You'll be walking through four cars," the conductor explained. "In the last car, you'll have to climb down a ladder to the tracks. Someone will be there to help you. We've got a ways to walk on the tracks, folks, and it's dark out there. Stay away from the third rail. It's the one that's raised and is way over to the side of the track. We won't be anywhere near it, but keep it that way. Because if the power comes on and you touch it —"

"Zap!" said Smoking Guy. He sounded mean. "There're a few people here I'd like to introduce to the third rail."

The little boy hid behind Mandy's leg.

Carolyn put her backpack on her sweaty shoulders and helped Rose up. Mandy, she noticed, was holding Todd's hand. Maya carried his baby sister's folded stroller so his mother could carry her. Joy was helping the girl who'd been crying.

They moved slowly through four hot and airless subway cars before reaching the door at the front of the subway. Carolyn was following Rose down the ladder into the tunnel when Smoking Guy called out, "Careful for the rats."

A few screams.

Someone said, "I'm not going down there."

Carolyn froze. *Rats!* She'd seen rats scurrying around the tracks. Thousands, she knew, lived in the subway tunnels. Maybe hundreds of thousands.

A subway worker signaled with his flashlight. "Let's go, miss. There are a lot of people behind you."

When Carolyn touched ground, Rose patted her

arm. "Don't worry, dear. Let's just be glad we're finally going to get out of here." Carolyn took her elbow and they joined the march through the dark tunnel.

"You can use your cell phones for light," a voice behind Carolyn called out. Mandy!

Maya stepped into darkness dotted with stars of cell phone lights.

Mandy handed her camera to Joy. "Could you shoot for me? I don't want to let go of Todd."

"It's too dark to shoot," observed Joy.

"The camera has a night-vision feature," Mandy said. "It's already turned on."

Joy looked through the lens and saw everything around her in an eerie green light. She focused on the young girl and asked, "What's your name?"

Close-up of girl saying, "My name is Helen Yee."

Zoom out for a long shot of the dark tunnel behind Helen Yee.

People walking at a slow, careful pace.

Smoking Guy pushing to get ahead of the people in front of him.

Zoom in. Mandy holding Todd's hand and turning to say something to his mother.

"How far do we have to walk?" someone shouted.

"Six blocks," a woman who was helping called back.

To Joy it seemed like they'd walked a lot farther than that when cheers broke out ahead of them. "We must be getting closer," a man behind her said.

As they inched slowly through the darkness, daylight filtered down from a square opening in the roof of the tunnel. A set of steep stairs reached up to the light and the street above them. A stern-looking transit authority officer stood at the foot of the steps. "Now take it slow, folks," he instructed in a gruff, tired voice. "You're almost there. We don't want any broken bones."

One by one, they climbed up the metal ladder.

Carolyn stepped out into daylight and blinked at the sudden brightness. She watched her friends and the people they were helping come out. They were sweaty and smudged with dirt from walking through the tunnel.

Mandy gave what was left of her water to Rose.

Maya opened the stroller for the young mother.

Joy tried to get a signal on her cell phone so Helen Yee could call her mother.

The streets were mobbed with people — some were walking, others clustered in little groups listening to transistor radios. Cars and trucks moved slowly on the street. Carolyn noticed that the traffic lights weren't working.

Rose patted Carolyn's arm. "I can walk home from here. Thank you."

Before Carolyn could say anything, Rose merged with the crowd walking downtown. "I need to call my dad," Carolyn said to anyone who was listening.

Joy snapped her phone closed. "My cell's not working."

Mandy came out of the deli on the corner with small bottles of water.

"The power is out all over the East Coast — all the way into Canada," Mandy reported. She handed water to Carolyn, the young mother, Helen Yee, Maya, and Joy. Joy handed hers to a sweaty elderly man coming out of the subway emergency hatch.

"They don't know what caused the blackout," Mandy continued, "but they say it's *not* terrorists. Anyway, no lights until sometime tomorrow. "

Carolyn turned to Todd's mother. "How are you going to get home?"

The woman looked around. "Walk, like everyone else. I don't live so far." Todd was already standing on the riding platform attached to the stroller. "We're walking *all the way home*," he announced proudly.

Mandy and Carolyn exchanged a grin.

The young mother thanked them, wished them good luck, and joined the crowd moving uptown.

"Should we start walking, too?" Maya asked.

Helen Yee grabbed Joy's hand. "Don't worry," Joy told her. "We won't leave you alone."

"Where do you live?" asked Maya.

"In the Bronx," the girl answered in a shy voice.

Joy looked at Mandy and Carolyn. How would they get Helen Yee all the way to the Bronx?

"What were you doing when you got on the train?" Mandy asked. "Were you visiting someone?"

"I stayed with my grandma last night."

Carolyn asked where the grandmother lived.

"On Canal Street."

"Near the subway stop?" asked Joy.

The girl nodded.

"So we can walk you back there," added Maya. "Your grandmother knew you were on the subway. She must be worried about you."

And my dad must be worried about me, thought Joy. My mom, too. And what about Jake? Are he and Sue stuck on an elevator somewhere? Or worse, were they in the subway? Are they still on a train?

"I need to find out if everything's okay at my dad's," Joy announced. "He lives near here."

"I'll take Helen to her grandmother's," offered Maya.

"Great idea," agreed Mandy. "I'll go with you. Carolyn can go with Joy."

"Then we'll meet you at your dad's, Joy," suggested Mandy. "Just tell me where."

Joy gave them the address of her dad's new apartment. As she said it, she remembered that she hadn't told her friends that her dad had moved. It was too late to take it back. "Apartment 12F."

Carolyn pointed the water bottle at her. "I thought your dad lives on West Broadway."

"Not anymore," Joy said sharply. "They moved." She didn't tell them that it was a smaller, not-as-nice apartment. They'd see that for themselves.

Mandy, Maya, and Helen Yee walked south, while Carolyn and Joy joined the crowds moving west. At every corner, Carolyn tried to call her father from Joy's cell phone. No luck.

Dad, be okay. Please be okay.

"My dad lives on the twelfth floor," Joy announced when they reached his new apartment building.

The stairwell was dark, but there was a little light coming in through a narrow window on each landing.

Joy stopped to catch her breath between the fifth and sixth floors. "If the lights don't go on before tonight, it's going to be really dark in here."

The door to the apartment was locked. "I don't have a key yet," Joy explained as she tried the buzzer. It didn't ring. "Must be electric," she said. She knocked.

Her father opened the door. "I was so worried about you," he said as he wrapped his arms around Joy and hugged her.

Jake grabbed Joy around her leg. "Oy! Oy!"

She lifted him up and hugged him hello. "We were on the subway," Joy told her father.

"That's what I was afraid of," he said as they followed him into the living room and sat on the couch. Jake leaned his sweaty head against Joy and sucked on his bottle.

"Where were you guys when the lights went out?" Joy asked her father. She looked around. "Where's Sue?"

"She's lying down," he answered. "Recovering from her ordeal."

"What ordeal?" asked Joy.

"Tell me where you were first," he said.

Joy and Carolyn told him the story of being

stuck on the subway and how they'd finally gotten out. In the middle of it, Sue came in from the bedroom.

"Thank goodness you're all okay," she said when the girls had finished.

"What happened to you?" Joy asked.

"I was coming back from grocery shopping with Jake. The lights went out. The elevator didn't work."

"You were on it?" exclaimed Joy. "With Jake?"

"How'd you get out?" asked Carolyn.

"She was not on the elevator," Joy's father answered for Sue.

"I was about to get on the elevator," Sue explained. "It's lucky we weren't, because the woman who was on it got stuck there for more than an hour. I walked up twelve flights of stairs carrying a squirmy twenty-pound child." She shot an angry look at her husband.

"While I was here looking for batteries and candles in case the blackout goes into the night. Which it seems to be doing."

"Thank you dear," Sue said sarcastically. "Didn't you, for one second, wonder how I was going to get home? Didn't you, for one second, think of coming to look for us?"

He scowled. "You seem to forget I was going down the stairs to look for you when I met you on the tenth floor."

"That was a big help," mumbled Sue.

Joy looked pleadingly at her father. Why did they

have to fight all the time? Why did they have to do it in front of her friends?

"The important thing is that we're all safe," he said in a calmer voice. "We have some fresh fruit pops in the freezer. That might cool us off."

"I'll get them," said Sue turning toward the kitchen. "I burned enough calories walking up to deserve one myself." Meanwhile, Joy's father went to look out the window.

Carolyn was thinking about her own dad. Where was he? Was he stuck on an elevator? Wherever he was, she knew he was worried about her, too. She leaned toward Joy. "I'm going home as soon as Maya and Mandy get here. Even if we have to walk all the way."

"I'll go with you," Joy whispered back. "If my dad will let me."

He'd opened the window. "It's even hotter outside," he observed as he closed it.

Jake had fallen asleep leaning on Joy. She carefully laid his head on the couch cushion. Now was the time to ask her dad.

"Can Joy walk uptown with me?" Carolyn asked suddenly. "Can she stay overnight at my apartment?"

Joy shot her a grateful glance before adding, "It will be easy for me to go crosstown to Mom's tomorrow from Carolyn's."

"You're going to walk all the way uptown?" he asked.

Joy stood up. "Everyone's doing it. It's the only way to get around. Can I, Dad?"

He nodded his agreement. "I'll try to reach your mother and tell her you're okay."

She leaned over and kissed Jake. "Thanks, Dad. We'll wait for Mandy and Maya downstairs so they don't have to walk up."

Joy and Carolyn took their frozen pops, said good-bye, and headed down the stairs.

"Be careful, girls," her father called after them. "And, Joy, call me as soon as you can."

They met Mandy and Maya between the third and fourth floors. Mandy walked down the rest of the stairs next to Joy. "Thanks for shooting for me in the tunnel, Joy. I checked it out. It looks great."

"It was fun," admitted Joy.

Every five blocks Carolyn tried to call her father. Phone calls to Joy's mother and Maya's family didn't work, either.

Maya noticed a police car slowly passing by. "My dad must be so busy tonight," she said. "I hope people don't start looting. He said that happened during the last big blackout."

Mandy took out her camera again. "Look around," she said. "It's getting dark out, but *no* lights are going on."

Maya looked up at skyscrapers darker than the night sky. "There're always *some* lights on," she said. "It's eerie."

Carolyn pointed to a hotel lobby. People were sitting and lying around on the lobby floor. "There're lights in there."

"They must have a generator," commented Joy. "But I bet the elevators aren't working and that they don't have lights in their rooms."

"Or air-conditioning," added a cute guy walking near them.

"Good point," agreed Mandy with a smile in his direction. She grabbed Carolyn's arm. "Come on," she said excitedly. "I want to shoot the lobby through the window. This whole blackout is one great big photo opportunity."

Maya took out her camera. Joy, too. Carolyn dug into her backpack. Her camera was in there somewhere.

Carolyn took pictures of the hotel lobby and street scenes as they continued their hike through the darkness.

A long shot of Times Square without lights. Click.

A medium shot of people sitting on a curb waiting for a bus. Click.

A long shot of an outdoor café. People drinking, talking by candlelight. Click.

Close-up of Mandy with her video camera, her hair sticking to her head with sweat. Smiling. Click.

It was night. It was dark. It was hot. For block after block the only light they saw came from headlights of slow-moving cars and buses and the dim glow of candlelight in apartment windows. Bicyclists passed.

By the time they reached 60th Street, Carolyn had taken ten digital shots that she liked.

People were sitting in little groups, talking in low voices. A Korean deli was giving away bottles of water and sandwiches. The girls each took a small bottle.

"Open all night," the deli man called to them.

At 65th Street, Maya used a pay phone to try calling her family again. "I think it's working," she told Joy. "It is!" she exclaimed when she heard her grandmother's voice on the other end. "Grandma, it's me, Maya. I'm fine. I'm walking uptown with Carolyn, Joy, and Mandy. Is everybody okay?"

Carolyn could tell by the expression on Maya's face that her family was fine. When she hung up, she told Carolyn, "My grandma said I should stay at your place tonight. If that's okay."

"'Course it's okay," agreed Carolyn.

Then Mandy tried calling home collect. It worked. "They were really worried about me," she said as she hung up. Joy borrowed change from Mandy and tried calling her mother again, but still couldn't get through.

The closer Carolyn came to her street, the more frightened she became about her dad. When they finally reached the corner of 81st Street and Amsterdam, she started to run. Mandy ran beside her. Halfway up the dark block, Carolyn saw a man coming toward them with a flashlight. "Dad!" she yelled as she picked up speed to meet him.

He pulled her close in a hug. "I was *so* worried about you girls," he murmured. She could hear the tears in his voice.

"I was worried about you, too, Dad," she said through her own happy tears.

Joy, Mandy, and Maya caught up.

"We walked all the way from downtown," Joy bragged.

Carolyn's father looked at his watch by the beam of the flashlight. "It's nine o'clock," he said. "It took you that long?"

"We were stuck on the subway for a little while," explained Mandy.

"Like, for more than an hour," added Joy.

"I was afraid of that," he said. "You must have been frightened."

Carolyn leaned against her father's side. "Just a little." He put his arm around her shoulders.

Mandy walked backward and shot them walking.

I would have been more frightened in the subway if Mandy hadn't been there, Carolyn realized.

As they continued up the block, her father asked if the other girls had been in touch with their families.

Maya reported that she'd spoken to her mother, and Joy said her father and Jake were okay. Mandy said she'd called home, too. "But I haven't been able to reach my mother," Joy added.

"Call her at your apartment number instead of her cell phone," Dr. Kuhlberg suggested. "It's mostly land lines that are working."

They reached the front of the building. A dozen or so people were sitting around — some of them in lawn chairs, some right on the sidewalk. Emergency candles were lined up against the building and along the gutter. A folding table was covered with paper plates, plasticware, and bread. Two outdoor grills were going.

"It's an impromptu party," Dr. Kuhlberg explained. "People are bringing meat and fish from their freezers."

"We should eat it," said a man at the grill. Carolyn read his apron: DO NOT DISTURB. GENIUS AT WORK.

Dr. Kuhlberg reached through the open window to the first-floor apartment and pulled out a phone and handed it to Joy. "The super's been letting everyone use it," he explained. "It's connected to the wall, so don't walk away with it." He smiled.

Joy dialed the apartment. Her mother answered on the first ring. "Where are you?" she asked in a frightened voice.

Joy told her the whole story.

Carolyn poked her on the back and whispered, "Ask her if you can sleep over."

Joy asked and smiled her mother's answer to Carolyn. Next, she called her dad.

"Where were you when the lights went out?" Mandy asked Dr. Kuhlberg.

"In the elevator," he said calmly.

"You were!" exclaimed Carolyn. "That's what I was worried about. What happened?"

Mandy turned her camera back on and focused on him.

Dr. Kuhlberg looked directly into the camera. "Actually, I had quite an adventure. It's worth recording."

West 81st Street

"Were you alone on the elevator?" Maya asked Carolyn's dad.

"No."

"Who else was with you?" Mandy asked.

"How did you get out?" added Joy.

A little shiver ran through Carolyn. It was scary to be stuck on the subway but worse to be stuck in an elevator.

"I got on the freight elevator to take our laundry up from the basement," her father began. "Miss George entered on the first floor with one of the dogs she walks. The *largest* dog she walks. Precious."

Carolyn noticed Ivy and a dark-haired woman coming out of the building. Ivy was carrying a large bowl. "We have a salad," the dark-haired woman announced. When Ivy saw Carolyn she put down the bowl and ran over to her. Carolyn didn't know if Ivy had tears of relief in her eyes or if her eyes were just sparkling in the candlelight.

"We were so worried about you, Red. Where were you?"

"On the subway," Joy and Maya said in unison.

"Tell me about it," said Ivy.

"You tell first," said Mandy as she turned the camera on Ivy. "How did you get out of the elevator?"

"How did you get Precious out?" added Maya.

Ivy turned to Carolyn's father. "You tell, Donald."

Carolyn exchanged a look with Mandy. *Donald!*

In the end "Donald," Ivy, and Mr. Santos — the superintendent of the building — told the story together. How the elevator stopped between floors. How Mr. Santos — the first hero of the story — climbed down through the elevator shaft to the roof of the elevator. "I open the hatch," Mr. Santos explained. "I put in ladder and Miss Ivy climbs out."

"What about Precious?" asked Carolyn. "He can't climb a ladder." She turned to Ivy. "Can he?"

"No," laughed Ivy. "That's where your dad came in with his wonderful idea. He's the second hero in our story. He was brilliant."

"Not so brilliant," protested Dr. Kuhlberg.

"He made a sling with one of the big towels from his laundry," explained Ivy.

"He put it under big dog's belly," Mr. Santos said, picking up the story. "Picks up big dog. Miss Ivy and me take ends of towel and pull. Out comes dog."

"Precious was *so* good," Ivy said. "He knew it was an emergency and was as calm as calm could be." She smiled at Carolyn's father. "Just the way you were."

"Come and get it," the guy at the grill shouted.

After they ate, some people drifted back to their apartments. But a dozen or so stayed outside on chairs and some crates that Mr. Santos brought up from the basement. Ivy put the candles on one of the crates, and they all moved their seats to form a semi-circle around the light.

Carolyn glanced up and down the block. Some apartment windows and the front of a few other buildings had flickering candlelight. Otherwise the street was dark.

Ivy looked up at the dark, star-studded sky. "No planes."

"The airports are closed," Mandy said in a hushed voice. "I hadn't thought about that."

"This night is so still," continued Ivy. "I've never played music in total stillness."

"Would you drum for us now?" asked Dr. Kuhlberg.

"I'd love to," answered Ivy. She was already looking around for something to play. Carolyn handed her the empty metal salad bowl. Ivy pulled over a crate and put the turned-over bowl on it.

"How about this?" asked Maya, holding out an oversized fork hanging from the side one of the grills.

Ivy wiggled her fingers in the air. "I'll use my hands." She started out with a soft, slow, persistent beat then added rhythms and little vocal pops and clicks.

After playing for a while, Ivy suggested they all sing. "How about some country music from Carolyn and Mandy to start us off?"

Carolyn and Mandy sang two cowboy songs that Carolyn's grandfather had taught them. Both songs had easy-to-learn choruses, so everyone could join in. While they sang, Carolyn looked into the candlelight fire. It's like our campfires at the ranch, she thought — talking and singing in the night. Me and Mandy.

When they finished, Mandy leaned close and whispered, "It's like our campfires back home."

Carolyn nodded and smiled. She didn't have to tell Mandy she was thinking the same thing. Mandy already knew that.

Joy sang a song she learned at sleep-away camp about the old lady who swallowed a fly. A lot of people knew it, and the others learned it as they sang along. Dr. Kuhlberg sang a song he learned during one of his trips to South Africa. Ivy added percussion.

After singing for a long time, they told their stories all over again about where they were when the blackout happened. This time, everyone took their time and gave more details. Mr. Santos admitted that he was really afraid they wouldn't be able to get Precious out. And Maya said that she'd been afraid that Smoking Guy would do something stupid and dangerous.

"He was really angry," agreed Joy.

Around two in the morning, Ivy announced that she was going home.

The dark-haired woman said Ivy could sleep

over in her apartment. "You'll just have to come back in the morning to walk the dogs, anyway," she added.

Ivy stood up. "I need to go home and check on my bird. I don't have to walk the dogs tomorrow — no one's going to work."

Dr. Kuhlberg stood up, too. "I'll walk you, then."

"Donald, you can't walk me," protested Ivy. "I live on a Hundred and Eighty-second Street. That's five miles from here. Besides, I have my bike." She smiled at him. "But thank you."

"I'll borrow a bike and ride with you," he said.

"Then you'll be riding alone coming back."

"We can't let you go alone," he protested.

Ivy put a hand on his arm. "You're going to have to, because that's what I'm going to do."

Her hand was still on his arm. He patted it. "All right, then. But I still don't like it."

Maya and Joy exchanged a glance. Was Operation Romance happening without them?

Does Ivy actually *like* my dad? Carolyn wondered. Like as a *guy*? Will they go out on dates?

After Ivy left, the girls and Dr. Kuhlberg took candles and walked up ten flights of stairs in the flickering light. When they reached the apartment, they put two of the candles on the kitchen counter. Carolyn's dad took one to his room, the girls had two for Carolyn's room.

Joy stretched out on the rug between the bed and the door. "I'm sleeping right here."

"You can have my bed," offered Carolyn.

Joy yawned. "The floor is fine. I'm so tired I could sleep standing up."

Carolyn gave her a clean sheet, her extra pillow, and the quilt from her bed to fold up for a mattress. It was so hot in the apartment that no one needed a blanket. Maya put the cushions from the living room couch in the little space between Mandy's pullout and Carolyn's bed.

An hour later Carolyn was still awake, listening to Joy's soft snores and going over and over in her head all that had happened to them that day. She slipped out of bed, stepped over Joy, and went to the kitchen for something to drink. She found a warm ginger ale in the dark refrigerator, popped it open, and sat at the counter to drink it.

"I couldn't sleep, either," a voice whispered from the darkness. Mandy. She sat at the counter across from Carolyn. Carolyn pushed the can of soda toward her to share.

Mandy took a sip and pushed the can back. "I'm going to make my video about the blackout instead of my trip of New York City. Just the blackout."

"You're not going to use all that other stuff you shot?" asked Carolyn.

"Maybe I'll use the footage of Times Square when it was all lit up. You know, to show the difference from when it was dark during the blackout. I don't mean that you weren't good on the tape. You guys were all good sports about my video. Well, maybe not Joy." Mandy lit the three candles on the counter. "But the blackout. That's a big story. And I was here. It's okay to change what it's about. Don't you think?"

"I think it's a good idea," said Carolyn.

"You hungry?" asked Mandy.

"Yeah. I am."

Carolyn took a jar of peanut butter and a loaf of bread out of the cupboard.

Mandy used one of the candles to find a knife in the silverware drawer and handed it to Carolyn. "Remember how we used to sneak to the kitchen in the middle of the night and make peanut-butter sandwiches?"

Carolyn smiled to herself. "I was just thinking about that." She pictured them in the moonlit kitchen at the ranch. That was with the old Mandy. This was the new Mandy, with bleached hair, a hip wardrobe, and all the confidence in the world. "You've changed a lot, Mandy," she said.

"You've changed, too," said Mandy. "That's what I was most afraid of."

Carolyn glanced up from spreading peanut butter. "Huh?"

Mandy was looking into the candlelight. "You changed a lot when you moved to New York," she explained. "It showed in your postcards and e-mails. You were so excited about meeting new people and all the great things you were doing. I saw it when you came home to visit, too. You even dressed different. I was afraid I'd embarrass you. That I'd be, like, this country bumpkin."

"I dressed different because I started going to Remember Me." She spread peanut butter across another slice of bread. "You changed the way you dress even more. Why didn't you tell me about Katrina and dyeing your hair and everything?"

"I didn't think you'd care," said Mandy. "You had all your new friends."

Carolyn thought Mandy sounded a little angry. She checked her out in the flickering candlelight. She didn't look angry. She looked sad. "Of course I cared. You were my best friend. I was homesick. I missed you. I was looking forward to your coming to the city so much. Then when you got here it was like you were a" — she paused before quickly completing the thought — "a stranger. You just wanted to do whatever you wanted to do and didn't care about anybody else."

"I wanted to be a city girl," explained Mandy. "Like you guys. I thought we were all having fun doing city stuff. Maybe not Joy all the time. But you, me, and Maya."

Carolyn could hear the hurt in Mandy's voice. How could she explain all this to Mandy without hurting her feelings even more?

"It was fun a lot of the time," she agreed. "We just didn't want to do so much. When you live here you don't do touristy things every day. Anyway, we couldn't keep up."

"You guys are so close," said Mandy. "I felt like an outsider sometimes."

Carolyn put a sandwich on a napkin and placed it in front of her. "It's hard being the new person coming into a group," she said quietly. "Don't feel bad. You really did great. When I moved here, I was so shy at first."

They each took a bite of sandwich. "I missed you, C-Sis," Mandy said softly. "I cried so much after you left. Everything was different. I didn't even like riding anymore. Everything was new and exciting for you. But for me it was the same old things, only without my best friend."

"I missed you, too," admitted Carolyn. "And the ranch. I still miss it. And you."

"Even though you've changed?" asked Mandy. "Even though *we've* changed?"

"I don't think we've changed that much," said Carolyn. "We're still the same deep down."

Neither of them said anything for a minute. Mandy broke the silence. "I couldn't sleep because I kept thinking about everything that happened today. I was really scared on that subway. I would have been a lot more afraid if you hadn't been there, C-Sis."

"Me, too," admitted Carolyn. "I would have been a lot more afraid if *you* hadn't been there, M-Sis."

"Maybe you should use the blackout for your workshop project," suggested Mandy. "You took lots of pictures when we were walking."

"I'm doing my project on you," Carolyn said, having the idea as she said it. "It will be close-ups of you from all the years we've been friends. I have all your school pictures. They'll all be in it. In rows. And I'll use a picture of you now — maybe with your video camera. I'll have that big, over all the other shots. What do you think?"

"You always have good ideas," said Mandy.

"You, too."

Mandy's face glowed in the candlelight. She looked at Carolyn and smiled. Her dimples were in shadow, but Carolyn could still see them.

"Did you want jam on your sandwich?" Carolyn asked suddenly.

Mandy looked down at her sandwich minus one bite. "Is it too late?"

"It's never too late," Carolyn told her.

Joy was the first to get up the next morning. Dr. Kuhlberg was in the kitchen. "Good morning," he said cheerfully. "I'm making breakfast." He gestured toward the counter where breakfast was laid out — a big jar of applesauce, a box of raisins, the rest of the loaf of bread that Carolyn had opened, peanut butter, strawberry jam, three bananas, and a quart of apple juice.

Maya came into the kitchen. She was already dressed. "I'm going to start walking home," she announced.

"Not until you've had breakfast, young lady," Dr. Kuhlberg said in his father voice.

While the girls ate their blackout breakfast, they

talked about the cookout and candlelight campfire and how much fun they'd all had.

Carolyn and Mandy told stories about campfires and camping trips in Wyoming. For the first time Maya could see what a wonderful friendship Carolyn and Mandy had. She leaned closer to Joy and whispered, "Look how happy Carolyn is."

Joy nodded and thought, Now I can see that Mandy and Carolyn are good friends. She remembered shooting for Mandy in the subway tunnel. It was fun. And I actually liked it when Mandy used my computer to edit. We had a good time together. Mandy isn't so bad.

Mandy told them her idea about making her fifteen-minute video about the blackout instead of about being a tourist in New York City.

They all thought it was a good idea. "You can edit it on my computer if you want," offered Joy.

"Actually, I want to go home to edit," said Mandy. She looked over at Carolyn. "I know I planned to stay longer, but I kind of want to go home as soon as I can get a flight."

"You're leaving?" exclaimed Carolyn. She was surprised at how disappointed she felt and thought, Twenty-four hours ago I wanted her to leave more than anything.

Maya and Joy exchanged a glance. Mandy was actually going home?

"You could edit it here and send it to the station over the Internet," suggested Joy.

"There's an editor at the station who's been teaching me," explained Mandy. "She'll help me make it really special."

Maya held up a hand. "Listen."

Joy heard a humming sound. "The refrigerator," she said. "The lights are back on."

Hoots and hollers came from the street below and through the open windows of nearby apartment buildings.

"The blackout is over," announced Dr. Kuhlberg.

A few minutes later, Joy and Maya left together. "Let's walk down in case the lights go out again," suggested Maya. "I don't want to be stuck on the elevator."

They started down the ten flights of stairs.

"So we got our wish," Joy said between the ninth and eighth floor.

"What wish?"

"That Mandy would leave," answered Joy. "Are you glad?"

"No. I like her."

"I didn't like her until yesterday," said Joy. "I guess I was kind of mean to her about the video."

"Mandy was a little pushy about shooting," agreed Maya.

"I can't believe that I want her to stay," said Joy as she opened the door. "I think I might even miss her."

"Don't worry," said Maya as she stepped out onto the street. "I have a feeling that she'll be back."

*   *   *

Two days later, Carolyn was sitting on her bed watching Mandy pack. "I'm going to miss you," said Carolyn.

"Me, too," agreed Mandy. She looked up at Carolyn over an armful of folded tops. "Katrina's okay. But it's not the same with new friends."

"I know." Carolyn held Mandy's soft suitcase open so she could drop in her clothes.

"I have an idea!" exclaimed Mandy. "Come back with me. You could stay for the rest of the summer. Your grandparents would love that. And we'd ride together. I'd ride again if you were there."

A thrill ran through Carolyn. Tailgate. The ranch. The open spaces and cool fresh air. Her grandparents. Mandy. "Maybe I can come at the end of the summer for two weeks or something," she said. "If I can get a cheap flight."

Mandy zipped her bag closed. "Perfect! By then my tape will be done. You'll meet Katrina. But we'll do stuff alone, too."

"Just the two of us," said Carolyn.

Mandy's eyes sparkled as the familiar smile spread across her face and dimpled her cheeks.

On the way back from the airport, Carolyn's father dropped her off at Joy's for a sleepover.

After the girls made and atc spaghetti with meat sauce and a salad, they gave one another pedicures and watched a cheesy horror movie. As Joy put the DVD back in its case, she asked Maya, "How's your project coming along?"

Joy turned on the computer and showed them the image that she'd created.

A shot of under Joy's bed overlaid with monster clip art. All around the edges, a repeated close-up of a Joy screaming in terror.

"That's scary!" said Carolyn.

"I had a nightmare like that," added Maya with a shiver. She thought about her own project. Joy had helped her make it just right with Photoshop.

"Here's Maya's," Joy said as she brought the image up on the screen.

Medium shot in bright colors of a swing in motion overlaid with black-and-white long shot of three-year-old Maya running toward the viewer.

"I decided not to use the picture of the market," Maya explained.

Carolyn studied the image. "It's beautiful," she said softly. "I love how it feels like the swing is moving. And you can tell it's a memory because of the girl being in black and white. It gives the whole picture an old-fashioned look."

"Do you have an idea yet?" Maya asked her.

Carolyn described her idea. "All the pictures I'll use are close-ups of Mandy," she concluded. "I'll call it *Close-Up of My Closest Friend.*"

"It's a perfect idea," commented Maya.

While Joy and Carolyn opened up the sofa bed

and put on the sheets, Maya took their dishes to the kitchen. Carolyn and Mandy are still best friends even though they're both changing, thought Maya. Why can't Shana and I be like that?

Joy looked around her big room. There was a double bed, a convertible couch, a big TV on a stand, a bureau, a desk, and three big windows. This apartment is expensive, she thought, and Mom's business is in trouble. Will we have to give up this apartment, too? Will I go from having two bedrooms to having none?

A pillow hit her in the stomach. "Why so glum, chum?" asked Carolyn.

"Another Grandpa-ism, no doubt," shouted Joy as she threw the pillow back at her.

It hit a standing lamp instead of Carolyn and the lamp toppled. Carolyn grabbed it before it hit the floor.

Meanwhile, Joy swung around and threw the other pillow at Maya as she came through the doorway.

Maya threw it back at Joy.

Carolyn added her pillow to the action.

Three good friends having a pillow fight. Click.

Jeanne Betancourt lives and writes in New York City. She has written more than 60 books, including *My Name Is ~~Brain~~ Brian, Ten True Animal Rescue Stories*, and the popular Pony Pals series. Jeanne's work has been honored by many Children's Choice Awards. She is also an award-winning scriptwriter and has taught filmmaking to teens. Learn more about her at: jeannebetancourt.com.

Trista Sordillo